FOSSIL COVE PRESS

Winnipeg, Manitoba

THE FALL OF ATLANTIS

and

Other Exotic Speculations

by

D. G. Valdron

THE FALL OF ATLANTIS and Other Exotic Speculations

FOSSIL COVE PUBLISHING, 1301-90 Garry St., Winnipeg, Mb, Can, R3C 4J4

Issued in ebook and print formats
ISBN: 978-1-7771551-3-1 (ebook)
ISBN: 978-1-998453-24-5 (ingramspark print)

Text set in Garamond

D.G. Valdron's web site can be found at: denvaldron.com

THE FALL OF ATLANTIS
and Other Exotic Speculations
Table of Contents

The Rise and Fall of Atlantis

Reality Check

All right, first things first. Atlantis never existed. Nope. Uh uh. No way. Totally, fabricated. It's a story made up by Plato.

And it's obviously a story made up by Plato. You can read it for yourself. Plato tells the story in the form of a dialogue. He runs across an old pal, and they have a discussion. In the course of the discussion, Plato mentions Atlantis. What is Atlantis?

Plato then explains that it is an old and well known story that everybody knows, except that no one knows it. Plato then says he got the story from Solon father of Athens, so you know it must be true, even though no one has heard of it and Solon didn't mention it to anyone else. Then Plato says it's totally a real story, because he got it from the Egyptians, who know practically everyone, so it must be true. Plato then goes into a detailed and rather fanciful description of Atlantis, its geography, flora and fauna, and the fact that they worship all the same gods that the Greeks do, so all that detail makes it totally true, plus having the same gods - because the Gods are totally real. If he'd said the Atlanteans worshiped their own pagan gods, well, you'd know it was put on, because those gods are fake.. He describes the government of Atlantis, which turns out to be the same as Plato's ideal state, so that's got to be true. Then he said that the Atlanteans made war on Athens, which is why all the Athenians know about it and so do the Egyptians so it must be totally true, even if no one else remembers it. The gods destroyed Atlantis, because Athens was so rocking. The end!

The Fall of Atlantis – Page 1

Look, anyone who has read a post-Arthur Conan Doyle story recognizes what's going on. Before you get into the story, there's this elaborate dog and pony show about finding the manuscript in an old chest of drawers, or some beggar passing you a mysterious key, all of which is designed to gin up a provenance for the story that goes beyond 'I just made it up now.'

The Greeks didn't even care one way or the other. They weren't big on little details of whether something was true or not. Atlantis didn't really become a thing until the modern day, when people got obsessed and started looking for it all over the place. News flash, there are lots of buried cities, lost civilizations, extinct cultures, and they're fascinating and should be explored. But calling them Atlantis is a bit much.

So this whole thing is a thought experiment. We're going to create Atlantis, as realistically as we can get away with.

Where Would We Put a Lost Continent?

First problem is, where do we put it? In the Atlantic obviously. It's Atlantis, after all. So let's find a map of the Atlantic Ocean sea floor and start there. Preferably you want a topographic map, to give you a sense of how high or how low.

The trouble is, it's actually pretty flat. There's no actual suitable sunken land mass in the Atlantic that would serve the purpose. Back in the ice age when sea levels were a lot lower, there was a lot more land exposed, but this was just continental shelf.

But there's no actual sunken continents out there, no mini-continents, no micro-continents, no continental fragments. We have them in the Indian and Pacific Oceans, but not here.

There are islands and island clusters, but mostly, they're just sea mountains, not sunken or rising continents.

What we have to work with is the mid-Atlantic ridge. This is a chain of mountains that runs north to south, right down the middle of the Atlantic sea floor, like a giant zipper. The Atlantic Ridge is formed by the continental drift of North and South America going west, and Europe and Africa drifting east. As the sea floor widens, a trench opens up in the center, and magma builds up forming chains of mountains along the trench.

All of this is taking place very deep below us. The Atlantic Ocean floor is 4000 to 6000 meters down. In standard, that's 13,000 to 19,000 feet deep. The mountains tips of the ridge are pretty tall, averaging about 2500 to 3000 meters deep, only 6,000 to 8000 feet.

And there, right around the longitudes of Spain, beginning around Gibraltar, and stretching up to southern Ireland, on the one side, and northern New England, on the other, is one particular section of the Mid-Atlantic ridge that spreads out into a sort of skinny triangle, and actually rises high up. On the topographic maps, it looks like a big island, only 1500 to 2000 meters deep, about 5000 to 6500 feet. Only a mile under water, give or take. There's our Atlantis!

Of course, that's still under a mile of water. And we can't just remove a mile of water from the Atlantic, so we need to lift it up further. That's not out of the question. After all, this 'Atlantis' has already uplifted thousands of feet from the Ocean floor as part of the ridge. Iceland is another example of volcanic uplift, the Kerguelen plateau in the Indian Ocean is a Texas sized uplift region which was above water for seventy million years. Places like the Galapagos, the Azores and Hawaii are products of local volcanism and volcanic uplift. And of course, Atlantis is already uplifted well above the Ocean floor, and above the rest of the Mid-Atlantic ridge.

So, how do we get Atlantis to rise up a little more?

Where and when does this Atlantis come from? I'm going to bet on the possibly the late Miocene, but more likely the Pliocene Era, because geologically, there were some interesting things happening with Pliocene tectonics. There were two big changes that occurred, which might make for an arguable impact on the Atlantic.

The first thing is the largest fender bender in the history of the world. India, or technically the Indian continental plate, which has been racing recklessly north, collides with Asia. The force of that collision (in slow moving geological terms) is so intense that it literally piles up the Himalayas. This is between 10 and 2.5 million years ago. In a sense, it's still going on today. Even more than that, Asia is pushed slightly north. Even now, the collision is still going on, India is still plowing north into Asia, and Asia's still forced north as well as moving in its own lateral direction.

Now, here's the thing. The Atlantic is an opening ocean. The Americas and Europe are still pulling away from each other. Most of the movement seems to be America going west. But I believe that Europe is somewhat moving east. The Urals (sic) are the mountain range produced by the European plate bumping uglies with the Asian plates.

So India hits Asia, altering its movement a bit, how does that affect Europe? Europe's eastward momentum meets a divergent sheering force. You get mountains of course. But you also get obstruction, maybe the European plate's progress halts, hiccups or reverses a bit. But the European plate is pretty heavy. So the underlying inertia transfers to someplace lighter and weaker, the oceanic floor. Until, of course, that underlying geological shockwave, or the inertia of impact, runs up against the mid-Atlantic ridge, where the Ocean floor is actually spreading and it has nowhere to go. It's now pushing against a countervailing force, the spreading of the ridge.

What happens then? Up it goes. A section of the mid-Atlantic ridge is forced way up as a result of the Indian/Asian plate collision and breaks the surface.

Now, it's possible I've gotten this slightly wrong, and Europe is moving some other direction. South maybe, or North, or even West. I don't thing that really matters. The Ural Mountains show that the European plate and Asian plate are in some degree of conflict or tension, and that a relatively minor change in orientation of the Asian plate, will have repercussions on the European plate, which will in turn have repercussions.

We're still in the realm of real world geology here. I'm speculating a bit far afield, but I believe that I'm loosely within our understanding of plate tectonics. The advantage of this is that real world geology applies to the rest of the continental plate tectonics, and we don't have to worry about any of that stuff butterfly stuff. At least, not at this point.

Instead, the single leap we are making, is that the stress forces of the Asia/India collision would eventually reach a point of relative weakness in the ocean floor crush, and produce an uplift region. This isn't even all that unreasonable, since this seems to be what produced Iceland and Kerguelen, neither of which, as I understand it, are derived from continental plates.

So the change may be something as subtle as a magma current moving a few degrees in the upper mantle or lower crust, which produces no other discernible real world effect.

Is it just India?

The Fall of Atlantis — Page 5

Nope, there's something else interesting going on about 3 million years ago in the Pliocene: North and South America join up. Why does this happen? Well, there's a shift in the Caribbean tectonic plate. The plate apparently moves east, or fails to move west as quickly as North and South America. As a result there's joining.

Now, what's interesting about that? Well, it seems to me that the Caribbean plate is moving or pressured in an easterly direction, so it's likely that there's underlying stress that extend to and pushes up against the mid-Atlantic ridge.

The joining of the plate and squeezing between North and South America is probably exerting pressure against the plate, as seen in mountain formations and uplifts, producing Mexican and Central American mountain ranges on one side, and the Caribbean Antilles and big islands on the other. I'd think some of that pressure would also transfer and potentially express against the mid-Atlantic ridge, at which point, it has nowhere to go.

Result? Uplift. So add them together, the Caribbean Plate movement/North and South America Joining, and the India/Asia plate collision are both putting pressure on different sides of the mid-Atlantic ridge. The result is basically uplift pressure, and the attempt of one side of the ridge to slide over the other side of the ridge.

But where the two sets of opposing forces overlap, where the uplift force is coming from two different directions, and neither side can slide over the other side, there's nowhere to go but up, and you get....

Atlantis. It's pretty fair sized. Eyeballing it, probably about the size of Spain or France. Let's call it a quarter of a million square miles.

And in pretty much roughly the right place, hopefully.

How's that sound?

Okay, so we've got a mechanism for Atlantis, and we've even got a time frame for Atlantis to happen. Roughly 2.5 to 4 million years ago. Let's say 3 to 3.5 million give or take a hundred thousand years or so.

Of course, this Atlantis is not stable. It's basically an uplift region of the Mid-Atlantic ridge, produced by the stress from two continental plates. It's probably going to sink again. But that will probably take another few million years. (For the record, I'm not a geologist. A real geologist, or seismologist, or tectonicologist would kick my ass six ways from Sunday. But I do believe that there's enough open and unanswered questions in planetary geology, and enough built in uncertainty, that this theory's got at least some seat of the pants arguability). Okay, so what next?

Well, for my next trick, we're going to fill Atlantis with stuff.

Flora and Fauna, Populating the Continent

Now here's the thing: Mid-Atlantic ridge uplift, only three million years old, left to its own devices, we're not going to get much, biologically speaking. The Atlantis uplift isn't a real continent, it's not a tectonic plate, and it hasn't ever been part of a continent.

Which means that there's very little in the way of opportunities for life to spread to it. On the rest of the earth, all our biology, our suites of plants and animals come from the joining and separation of continents, and the critters moving back and forth. You can't do that across 1500 miles of empty ocean. Atlantis may end up a pretty barren place. The only plants will be the ones that arrive in the guts of birds, are carried by wind, or are hardy enough to survive drifting across the ocean, that's going to be thin.

The really impressive biological laboratories, like New Zealand and Madagascar, started off with a good repertoire of flora, and then they had fifty million years of isolation or better. We don't got that, so the plants are going to be relatively non-diverse, probably lots of empty and unexploited plant niches.

Probably relatively poor soils because of the biological under productivity. It takes a lot to make good soils - decades or centuries of vegetation growing, dying and decomposing, and the right kinds of bacteria helping the process along, along with worms, annelids, insects, etc., none of which have an easy route.

As for animals. Well, maybe a bunch of insect species that come over as a result of windstorms or hurricanes, surviving the float on pieces of debris. That might evolve into possibly some super-sized cockroaches. You'll get Birds and Bats, they can fly over. It's a long way, and most species won't make it. But you might get long distance types making it and settling in - at best, you'd get a flightless pigeon the size of a turkey, or a flightless goose. Maybe a few lizards survive the float to drift over and that's about it.

Pretty much nothing in the fields of domesticable plant or animal species. Atlantis will be a relatively empty, impoverished and barren place.

Well, that's no fun at all.

The only way around that, is that sometime in Atlantis geological history, we have to connect it up with another land mass. Good News: Candidates are Africa, South America, North America and Europe! Bad news? None of them are especially close, and most of them are far enough off that we can write them off completely.

Ahh, but, if we go to the topographic map, or Google Earth, and poke around the vicinity of Spain (offshore), what do we find? We find a whole bunch of off again, on again, seamounts and ridges going this way and that, but definitely heading.... towards the Mid-Atlantic ridge. Heading, in fact, towards the place where we'd be expecting our Atlantis to make an appearance, three or four million years ago. But clearly, these are geologically active regions, at least somewhat vulnerable to stress.

Let's say that in our altered timeline, the forces that produce the Mid-Atlantic uplift that produce Atlantis, probably act on these already geologically active and uplifted regions. And as Atlantis rises, so too do the uplift regions extend to connect to Atlantis. So, we've got a land bridge! From Spain!

Now, the good news, or maybe the bad news, is that the land bridge probably doesn't last. It's most likely the result of the tectonic stresses that are produced by the India/Asia collision.

The trouble is, that those stresses culminate are eventually released, as ridge climbs over ridge, or as Atlantis rises. So even as Atlantis is rising, the land bridge connecting it to the Eurafrican mainland is probably sinking.

Now, geologically, this is probably happening pretty fast. Within a few hundred thousand years. In biology terms, that's pretty slow. More than long enough for life forms, both plant and animal, to colonize their way onto the land bridge, and to grow all along it, even into the rising Atlantis.

What this means is that it's a one-time colonization event. The land bridge is relatively brief, and it's to a 'still rising' pseudo-continent. There's no two way exchange, there's no continuing colonization. Everyone has bought a one way ticket, and once they arrive, that's it, there's no more passages into Atlantis. Not until Man comes along.

So, what makes it to Atlantis? And what's it like now in our present day?

Well, basically, 3 million years isn't a really really long time to evolve radically, particularly when your population is confined to a relatively small pseudo-continent. Evolution is a factor of mutations. Mutations occur at a steady rate in a given population. You want mutations to occur faster, then you need a larger population - more population, more mutations occurring. You get more population by giving them more territory.

The other side of the coin is that if the land mass is fairly small - say instead of Asia or Africa, you just have a land mass the size of Spain, then it only sustains a relatively small population, which means fewer mutations occur. That means a much slower rate of change.

Evolution in Atlantis, with its quarter of a million square miles, is going to be relatively poky compared to an Island Continent of three to eight million square miles - Australia, South America and North America in its day. Or compared to the new world (North and South America) of 15 million square miles. Or EurAsiAfica of 35 million square miles.

On the other hand, in EurAsiAfrica, the threats to species will be coming from environmental conditions, and new competing plants and animals evolving in a series of habitats and biomes running over 35 million square miles. That's a lot of room for new species to evolve, and once they evolve to spread fast and become game changers somewhere else. In that much territory, it's easy for a new kind of grass, for instance, to evolve somewhere, spread like wildfire all over the place, cause the extinction of some lines of herbivores and trigger the evolution of new kinds of herbivores.

In Atlantis, you're not going to have new species showing up from the far corner of Asia. Instead, you get isolation and stability, instead of rapid replacement, existing species have more opportunity to adapt to changing conditions, or to simply reduce or alter their range. There'll be lots of local specialization, but very little of the revolutionary tug of war, which drives species into extinction.

So Atlantis becomes a sort of lost world of Pliocene flora and fauna, stuff that goes extinct back in EurAsiAfrica. You'll probably get some indigenous fine tuning - evolution doesn't stop entirely. But your plants and animals will basically resemble what was living in Europe and Africa three million years ago. Stuff.

So what do we have? Well, the Pliocene are the glory days of elephants. Poke around, and you'll find all sorts of Elephants and Elephant-cousins. There's the classical mammoth, found in North Africa, it might have been in the right place at the right time to make it to Atlantis. Maybe Mastodons. Perhaps Deinotheres, which were basically elephants with the tusks on the lower jaws.

Gomphotheres, a shovel tusked elephant, about the size of an Indian Elephant. Inhabited swamps and semi-aquatic habitats across Africa Europe and Asia. A likely land bridge traveler. The Gomphotheres were very successful, made it into North America, and may have survived in South America as late as 400CE. My take on it is that they were likely competing for habitat with the Hippos, but were also dedicated marshland creatures. Hippos probably won't make it to Atlantis, so the small marsh elephantoids might have the place to themselves.

I dunno, the notion of Atlantis as the last stand of the various elephant lines Appeals to me. They really were in full bloom in the Pliocene, and they got hit pretty hard through the Pleistocene, until by our time, there were only a couple of species left. But here, they'd survive. It might be interesting to see how broadly the elephant lines radiate with open niches and reduced competition. Perhaps we'd see a really slender gracile elephant, a kind of stick figure that takes the niche of Giraffes. Or potentially, small horse or cow sized fast running grazers. Evolution will be slow, but there might be some empty spaces to fill.

Chalicotheres, sort of crosses between gorillas and horses, with short hind legs, long fore legs, knuckle walking, and long claws. Morphologically, and possibly via habitat, they remind me a lot of the American sloths. They survived in Africa up until 2 million years ago, forest dwellers. I see them as solitary forest giants, sort of giant sloths/giant pandas/forest elephants. Their great claws and ability to rear up on hind legs would make them formidable.

If you want more conventional animals, then Psolea was a Roman nosed gazelle, which appears to have frequented Morocco and the Atlas Mountains in northern Africa, close enough to maybe make it across the land bridge. Lived up till 2.5 million years ago. It might have been the source of an adaptive radiation, so all the Atlantean gazelles might have had huge honkers. The Pliocene also have deer not too different from modern forms. Possibly, Libralcis, a big Pliocene deer that was native to France. Might have made it over the land bridge. Megaloceras, is another deer candidate. Want to go pack to more normal looking critters. There's a potentially domesticable cattle species that is in the right place at the right time.

What else? Cows and Antelopes are pretty likely. Hoofed ungulates were catching on back then. No giraffes by the way. Camels are coming into Asia from North America, they won't make it. Horses are a big maybe, I don't know what their range was.

Rodents, definitely. Cats definitely, including Scimitar Cats (not quite saber toothed), dagger tooth cats and actual saber tooths. Hyenas definitely.

Bears and Canines? They seem to have emigrated from North America during the Miocene, and by the Pliocene had spread widely. The famous Cave Bear, definitely found in Spain, goes back to the early Pleistocene, which suggests his ancestors had found their way already. There was also the bearlike Agriotherium.

Giraffes, while evolving, didn't seem to have made it into northern Africa or Europe. Rhinos favored Asia and North America, but seem to have been pretty sparse on the ground. My impression is that they didn't really hit their stride until the Pleistocene. Hippos also seem like a long shot, at best.

But it could get interesting. We can't necessarily assume that every single species makes it over. There may be gaps, and gaps mean vacant niches that the existing species that do make it over can exploit. I've speculated about Elephants perhaps moving into Hippo and Giraffe niches. But there may be other gaps that show up. For instance, if there's gaps in the Predator niches, then primates might move into some of them. In which case, Atlantis has killer apes or monkeys. There was actually one species of giant baboon, Dinopithecus, that was in North Africa, and could have made it over to become a successful killer monkey. Or maybe not. Something to think about.

We've definitely got successful lines of apes. Pliothecus was a sort of gibbon-like tree ape known from both Africa and Europe. It was likely in Spain and a good land bridge candidate. We also got apes. Apes and Monkeys. The Pliocene was the big golden age of speciation for Apes. There were maybe two hundred species worldwide, as opposed to the current handful (Gorillas, Chimps, Bonobos, Orangs, Gibbons and Humans). Apes and Monkeys ranged up into Southern Europe, were in Spain, so they probably made it over to Atlantis.

Want to have some fun? We might be looking at the loose time period where Australopithecus was getting into Homo Erectus. Now, Australopithecus doesn't seem to have ranged widely, but rather, stuck to his corner of Africa. On the other hand, Homo Erectus moves around quite a bit, and got all the way through Asia into Sundaland, but he seems a little late. It's barely possible that some intermediate species, like Paranthropus or Homo Habilis might well have made it into Atlantis before the land bridge sank.

Hominids were evolving pretty fast around that time, so we might well have seen some hominid speciation and new hominids in Atlantis - giants, trolls, goblins, dwarves, ogres, who knows. Or we might have a range of ape-men. Or we might have a parallel hominid, an Atlantean parallel human. That's a bit of a leap, since the Atlantean hominids are unlikely to evolve rapidly. But who knows... Perhaps the first local animal the Atlanteans domesticate are their own ancestors? Ape men? Or maybe they're just mysterious strange critters inhabiting the forests. Or powerful giant savages for the Colosseum.

Potentially, what we're going to see are the Eur-Asia-African species that are most prevalent in the region of Spain and North Africa crossing over on the land bridge. So it's going to be a snapshot of that area. A modern visitor to Atlantis would probably tend to see Atlantean fauna as resembling Africa, with some odd additions from Europe. But it's really genuinely archaic stuff.

The Fall of Atlantis – Page 14

Do you want Dragons in Atlantis? Well, there are a couple of
'gavial' type (long narrow snouted fish eaters) crocodilians in
the Pliocene that went up to 60 feet long. The only problem
is that the two known giant species are in South America, in
the Andes region, and India. But it's possible that a
population of the South American giants got trapped in the
Caribbean at the time of contact, and eventually wound up in
Atlantis. And if you want bizarre, one of the big South
American crocodilians (about 30 feet) went to filter feeding,
developing baleen plates instead of teeth.

Generally though, you won't get much fauna and minimal
flora from North or South America. It's just too far, there's
no possibility of a land bridge. The Supercrocs might be a
slim exception to the rule. But that's pretty much it. More
likely, Atlantean Supercrocs would be a parallel development,
if they existed at all.

North American fauna weren't going to get to Atlantis via a
sea route, but there was some possibility of North American
fauna getting into Asia and from there to Europe and
possibly Atlantis. I haven't studied up on the Bering
connection, but I'd guess that the linkage between North
America and Asia might have been connected to the
repercussions of the India/Asia impact. In which case, there
might not have been enough time for North American fauna
to have spread far enough to get into Atlantis. On the other
hand, the Land Bridge connection seems to have been an off
again, on again, sort of thing.

What else? I make Atlantis to be a pseudo-continent of
roughly a quarter million square miles. That's a lot of
territory. Islands tend towards dwarfing, and some of that
may happen here. My thinking is that while Atlantis is
comparatively huge, its hill and mountain character probably
creates a lot of isolated biomes and relative dwarfing. Expect
the river-elephant or shovel tuskers to probably downsize

from elephant sized to hippo/tapir sizes. On the other hand, the Chalicotheres, ranging widely in the forests and relatively undisturbed, may well grow to be much larger than on the continents, possibly up to the size of small elephants, just like the sloths. On the open plains of Atlantis, the biome is big enough that the giants will probably stay gigantic, or at least 80% original size.

The impact of humans on Atlantis' flora and fauna, when they show up, is probably not going to be good. On the one hand, my guess is that the fauna is going to be relatively robust, because it'll be experiencing strong seasonal change, lots of climactic shifts, and a pretty reasonable degree of indigenous predation. And the local species are relatively recently separated from Eurasia, so they might have a good chance to survive.

On the other hand, the North America and Australia precedents aren't all that good. 50/50 chances, basically (it is worth noting that a lot of the North American and Australian fauna did not succumb immediately, but held on quite a while, overlapping with humans in some cases for over 10,000 years in North America, and 30,000 years in Australia).

Humans might domesticate some Atlantean animals. I don't think that Atlantis gets horses. That seems like a real long shot to me. On the other hand, it's pretty clear that there are potentially domesticable cattle, antelope and deer. Primates of one sort or another may be a potential domestication candidate. I keep thinking Monkey Ninjas, but that's just me being bad.

But the really interesting possibilities are in the elephant lines. We know that in our own, both Asian and African Elephants were tamed and tamable. But Elephants were never truly domesticated because they live too long and take too long to grow up. Pregnancy lasts two years. An elephant takes 25 years to grow to adulthood. That's way too long. So early societies would basically tame wild elephants - in North Africa, in China, in Mesopotamia, in India and Southeast Asia. Most of these seem to have been independent taming events, suggesting that Elephants seem to be relatively easy to work with and are naturally tamable/domesticable. But anyway, because early societies wanted to avoid the work of raising elephants from babies, they'd just tame the wild ones. When the wild ones got hunted out, that was that for the Chinese, Mesopotamian and North African ones.

Atlantis may have a whole variety of Elephantoids that they can tame. And it's likely that there'll be smaller dwarf species that breed and grow faster, that might be conventionally domesticable. It's also possible that the Atlanteans may have a better husbandry technique, like the Lapp do with their semi-domesticated reindeer, and preserve wild populations for breeding.

Getting People to Atlantis...

Now, let's talk about the human impact. First step, of course, is getting a human impact.

On this model of Atlantis, we got lucky. This version of Atlantis is basically an uplift of the mid-Atlantic ridge caused by stresses of tectonic plates. It's a temporary phenomenon, Atlantis will eventually sink again.

As an isolated phenomenon, separate from any continent, this Atlantis should have been a home to nothing more complicated than a few lizard, various species of insects, and birds and seals.

But we got lucky, there was a transient land bridge from Spain, around three to four million years ago which allowed

Atlantis to be colonized by Pliocene flora and fauna. And that fauna and flora, isolated, without influxes of new species, big enough to offer stability, but small enough to slow the rate of chance, has become a 'lost world' of species that went extinct in our world.

Humans didn't make it into that lost world. The land bridge was too early. Homo Sapiens hadn't evolved. Hell, Homo Erectus hadn't evolved. There's a chance that Homo Habilis might have made it over, a remote chance. There's also a decent likelihood of colonization by multiple species of apes and monkeys.

But what about humans, real humans, or close enough....

Well, who are the candidates who might have made it to Atlantis?

I'm afraid that the odds are not good. All in all, humanity had a very poor record of getting out to and into the Atlantic Ocean Islands. Which is odd, because I can name at least three major sets of Island groups around the Atlantic, and all of them got settled heavily.

The first, of course was the Mediterranean, with its profusion of large and small Islands all along the way, from the Balearics and Sicily, Sardinia and Corsica in the west, to the Greeks, Crete and Cypress in the east. The Mediterranean produced a flurry of seagoing civilizations - the Greeks, Phoenicians, Egyptians, Romans, etc.

Oddly, the Mediterranean civilizations didn't spend a lot of time and effort venturing into the Atlantic. There were a few Phoenician expeditions along the coast of Africa. The Romans fiddled about in Britain. But that was about it. The Med was a placid friendly place full of rich and inviting shores. The Atlantic, in comparison, was an unfriendly Ocean, full of storms and giant waves, with desolate and uninviting shores. Mostly, the Mediterranean peoples gave it a pass.

Then there's the Caribbean - the Arawaks, etc. Obviously, these were people who knew how to Island hop. But mostly, the Caribbean Islands are laid out in a long string. Almost no Island is more than 100 miles from the next closest. Pretty much all of them, you can see the next Island. And of course, the sea is pretty tranquil. If there was a deep sea tradition for the Caribbean Indians, we have no record of it.

Finally, there was the Canadian Archipelago - including Greenland. A complex of seasonally frozen islands up north. These were pretty steadily and successively occupied. We have archeological evidence of Greenland being occupied from time to time as far back as 2500 years. But the Islands of the Canadian archipelago are pretty close together - even closer than the Caribbean. Most of them have multiple points where they come within 50 miles of each other, and in the winters, you can walk from one Island to the next. But they weren't deep water sailors either.

In fact, when you look at the record of actual discovery and settlement of the deep Atlantic Islands in our own time line, the record is pretty dismal.

Take Iceland. Iceland was a perfectly habitable place. Certainly much more habitable than Greenland. It was only a few hundred miles from Norway or Scotland, and in the direction of favorable currents. Yet Iceland seems to have remained unpopulated and untouched until the Vikings showed up. Now there's some suggestion that maybe Irish monks got there first, but if they did, they did jack all with the place and made no real impact. Earliest occupation of Iceland was around 800, and it didn't get serious till about a century later.

The Faroe Islands occupy a midpoint between Iceland, Scotland and Norway. But again, their settlement was relatively recent. The earliest occupation was around 400 AD to 600 AD - somewhat early, but you gotta remember that the Roman Empire was tits up by that time. Then a second wave, around 600 AD to 800 AD. The early inhabitants seem to have been the Celts. Then sometime after AD 800, the Vikings took over.

Further north - Svalbard and the Arctic Archipelagos remained completely uninhabited and undiscovered.

Further south it gets even worse, the Azores were vacant and unknown until the Portuguese stumbled across them. So were the Madeiras and Cape Verdes. All these Island groups remained uninhabited and largely unknown until the 13th and 14th centuries. St. Helena, in the middle of the Atlantic? Unknown until 1502. Bermuda, undiscovered until 1505. The Canary Islands were only 50 miles from the African mainland, in classical times were uninhabited. They seem to have been occupied by relatives of the Berbers sometime after AD 500. But again, they're only fifty miles out.

So this is our realistic range - roughly sometime after 400 AD, to about 1400 AD for the discovery and settlement of Atlantis. In practical terms the most likely period of actual initial settlement and discover would likely be around 700 to 900 by Celts and Norse respectively....

Again, that's no fun. Let's bend the rules a little bit.

So, who gets to Atlantis, when, and what are their chances. Let's evaluate the chances. After all, an uninhabited Atlantis may not be very interesting for storytelling:

1) 250,000 years ago - Neanderthals - Their chances? Not very good, I'm afraid, practically nil. The Neanderthals did pretty good - their range extended from Southern England,

Spain, Italy and Sicily, all the way through to the middle east and central Asia. But if you look at their range, they didn't go anywhere they couldn't walk. Sicily and Southern England were either connected to the land, or so close you could swim. Other big Mediterranean Islands... Neanderthals didn't get there - they're not in the Balearics, in Sardinia, Corsica, Cypress, etc. They made it to Southern England, but they didn't get to Ireland. It's hard to tell, but it doesn't appear that the Neanderthals had any boats or dugouts whatsoever, or any boating technology that would allow them to cross over. Now, we can always hand wave - maybe a group got stuck on an ice floe and got really lucky. But the odds are pretty long. If you did get Neanderthals to Atlantis, it would be a very very small group, possibly a single family, and if they did manage to survive, the population would have a rough time with lack of diversity and chronic inbreeding.

2) 40,000 years ago, give or take - Paleolithic Humans. Chances, slightly better than the Neanderthals, since we assume that they'll be more technically sophisticated and have a better survival toolkit. But not much better odds. Their route is about the same as for the Neanderthals - lots of luck. And their prospects are about the same.

3) 20,000 to 5,000 years ago - Mesolithic Humans - Chances? Still not very good, but not as close to nil. Slightly better than the Neanderthals though. Mesolithic humans appear to have had boats, likely dugouts, and they did engage in sea crossings. During the Mesolithic, we had settlement of Mediterranean Islands, and about 10,000 years ago, colonization of Ireland. With the Mesolithic, say about 5,000 to 10,000 years ago, we have the first real prospect for enough individuals to end up on Atlantis to form a genetically diverse population. Again, we're dependent on massive amounts of luck - but it's somewhat less ridiculous to imagine

that groups of Mesolithic boaters off the coast of Ireland or England might get swept out by currents or winds.

4) Mediterranean Archaic - Egyptians, Phoenicians, Greeks and Romans. Let's take them in term:

a) Egyptians - up to 5000 years ago. They were terrific sailors up and down the Nile. They may have sailed the red sea, and the eastern Med coast, and they commissioned the Phoenicians for some possibly more ambitious ventures. Unfortunately, their boats were rubbish, slow moving, required constant maintenance, and hugged the coasts. They never got very far. Next....

b) Phoenicians - up to 3500 years ago. Real deal, they sailed the whole of the Mediterranean, establishing cities as far out as Spain. Their most ambitious expeditions sailed along the African coasts, and there's even a rumor they circumnavigated the continent. On the downside, they didn't seem interested in going north, exploring the European coast, and may not have found England. They were pretty dedicated coast huggers and the Atlantic was nasty territory for them. Odds of finding Atlantis are still immensely long. The odds of settling it and having any kind of exchange are longer still. You might get Phoenician ships lost at sea stumbling across Atlantis, and perhaps the crew surviving there. But without womenfolk, there's not a lot of future. Beyond that, chances of getting there and getting back, even more remote. Chances of establishing a trading route or founding an organized settlement in communication with the Phoenician world... nil. Bottom line, the Phoenicians found the Canary islands, but they didn't find the Azores. Atlantis is just too far.

c) Greeks - on a par with the Phoenicians, and miles better than the Egyptians. But they don't seem to have left the Mediterranean much. They left that to the Phoenicians, their contemporaries and rivals.

d) Romans - say about 2000 years ago, give or take 500. Technically, they weren't much further along than the Greeks or Phoenicians. To their credit, they conquered England, discovered Ireland, and knew about the Canaries. But honestly, not very likely. About as feasible as the Greeks and Phoenicians. - i.e., possible, not probable.

Atlantis is just flipping hard to get out too. Let's bend the rules a little bit more....

The Cavemen of Atlantis

During the Ice Ages, between the coast of Spain and Atlantis, during the winter and spring, there is a seasonal gyre called the Ice Road, where the currents sweep out from Europe towards the Atlantean shore, piling up ice floes along the north east shores and islands of Atlantis.

Biologically, this had not resulted in any significant interchange. The currents of the ice road were unpredictable, prone to occasional strong surges which would tear apart sheets of sea ice and send them drifting north.

Over 250,000 years ago Neanderthal hunter/gatherer tribes along the Spanish and French coastlines engaged in a diverse seasonal subsistence economy. During spring, they congregated around rushing rivers and migration routes, killing migrating game, waterfowl and spawning fish. During summers they subsisted on small game, the occasional big kill, and gathering a multitude of plants. The hard time was winter, when the plants died, when everything was buried beneath snow and ice, when only the biggest game infrequently plowed through the drifts. Some Neanderthal tribes innovated by ice fishing in the cracks between ice floes. This lead to hunting the seals that used such cracks for breathing and would often haul out onto the floes for breeding.

The seal hunting strategy was risk but vital. Entire tribes would go out onto the ice. A good catch of seal could mean the difference between survival and starvation through the winter. But the ice was treacherous, over the years, many Neanderthals died when they stepped onto a thin patch of ice, or a fissure between floes opened suddenly.

On occasion an entire tribe could be lost when the 'Ice Road' current would surge, tearing apart floes and sending a stream of icebergs towards Atlantis. When this happened, the only chance of survival for the members of the tribe, drifting in the current, huddling together in their furs, with their handful of scrapers, gnawing at drying seal meat, and slowly poisoned by melting and drinking sea ice brine, was to reach Atlantis and somehow claw their way ashore.

Of those caught on the ice road somewhere between 97 and 99% simply died along the way, of cold and exposure, starvation, kidney failure, despair or drowning. Many never came near Atlantis, the current sweeping them into open sea, and the floe slowly melting or disintegrating beneath them until there was nothing to keep them from drowning.

But some survived to reach Atlantis. Many of those, of course, died after reaching the shores. Some survived to live and die alone. But the practice of bringing whole tribes out for the seal hunt meant that females, pregnant females and breeding pairs occasionally made it. From about 250,000 years ago, the Neanderthals colonized Atlantis, spreading through the landscape.

This was an Ice Age Atlantis which nonetheless sported a Pliocene flora and fauna, vanished from the rest of the world three million years ago. The northernmost reaches of Atlantis were glaciated of course, and a large belt of tundra persisted.

But in the south and central, the Pliocene landscape was holding on. The Neanderthals found this a genial world, as easy or easier to survive in than the one that they had left behind. Their tool kits adapted, their population density was somewhat greater than Europe's, but their genetic diversity was rather more narrow.

The Neanderthals were not alone in the Ice Age Atlantis. Homo Habilis, an earlier, more primitive species, was also there. Habilis, without competition from other homo, had not gone extinct. Rather, it had adapted to what had been marginal habitat for it, and then adapted further to the rigors of the Ice Age. Habilis had even diverged somewhat, into a small forest dwelling variety, averaging five to five and a half feet, existing in communal troops, and a larger, more solitary hill and mountain variety averaging seven feet and greater. These were not new homo species, any paleontologist or anatomist would have recognized the bones immediately as Habilis, what they were was akin to human races or dog breeds - a stream within the species.

The Large Habilis terrified the Neanderthals, and there were a number of conflicts. The mountain giants were driven further into the hills and mountains, becoming fierce and solitary, like the bears whose ecological niche they mimicked.

The smaller, forest dwelling Habilis slowly gave way to the Neanderthals, the two groups frequently avoiding and ignoring each other. But the Neanderthals were more efficient and effective, bit by bit, the Habilis were replaced and pushed to more marginal territories.

In the south, however, warmer temperatures and the lush diversity of the Pliocene ecology offered more bounty and more options. Neanderthal and Habilis groups frequently overlapped. Slowly, Habilis troops integrated within Neanderthal tribes, submitted to and found a place within the

dominance structures and hierarchies of the Neanderthal
society. Homo Habilis became the first domesticate, taking a
role roughly similar to dogs - companions, hunting assistants,
pack animals, and occasional harvested meat.

The Neanderthals of Atlantis did not change much. Their
relatively complex societies and tool kits, despite the
incorporation of Homo Habilis, largely resembled those of
their European counterparts. They were hunter-gatherers in
the summer, big game hunters in the winter. Proto-
agricultural practices emerged slowly, but nothing like true
agriculture or horticulture emerged. Semi-domestication of
micro-livestocks took place, but these moves were quite
tentative. The high point of Neanderthal technology and
science were the construction of fish traps in a few rivers and
streams.

In Europe, the Neanderthals went extinct, about 30,000 years
ago. The Neanderthals of Atlantis continued to thrive
however, untroubled by competition from modern humans.

It was not as if modern humans did not find their way to
Atlantis. As early as 50,000 years ago, hunters from tribes of
Paleolithic humans found themselves venturing onto the ice
for seals, much as their predecessors had. Some of them too
were caught on the unpredictable surges of the Ice Road.
Most of them died. Like the Neanderthals, a few made it.

The survivors were mostly males, breeding females were rare,
not unheard of but comparatively rare. This was a cultural
distinction. Human tribes had been larger, the females more
segregated, prone to be left alone and left behind during
hunting expeditions. The smaller more vulnerable bands of
Neanderthals had not had that luxury often travelled with
their females. So much fewer human females, and much less
opportunity for a distinct breeding population.

More critically, the shivering huddled survivors were not finding an empty landscape, but one already inhabited and dominated by Neanderthal tribes and their domesticates. Paleolithic and Mesolithic humans were never able to establish themselves as distinct populations in Atlantis, much less displace the Neanderthals.

Instead, the few that managed to survive, that did not die on route or on landing, that did not starve, that were not hunted down, the few that managed to incorporate into Neanderthal tribes contributed to Neanderthal culture and genome. Archeology would have shown a slow movement of new styles of tools and tool making in archeological sites, indicating occasional contact and transmission. The Neanderthal genome incorporated as much as 12 to 4 per cent of human DNA.

Homo Habilis did not interbreed with Neanderthals - not to say that copulation did not occur frequently. But the two human species were just a little too far apart to do more than produce the occasional mule. Nevertheless, Habilis survived in three distinct breeds, as reclusive and shy forest dwellers in niches like the African apes, as slaves/domesticates of the Neanderthals, and as savage mountain giants using agility and climbing ability to compete with rival bears, and strength and stealth against the Neanderthals.

As the Ice Age waned, ten thousand years ago, the Neanderthals of Atlantis rested easy in their island continent, oblivious to the fact that their race had passed away from the rest of the world, oblivious to the fact that the world was changing once again....

Arrival of the Atlanteans

Ten thousand years ago, give or take, the Ice Age comes to an end. The ice sheets retreat, the climate becomes warmer.

For Atlantis, this is a blossoming, as the Pliocene flora and fauna expands northward, reclaiming taiga and tundra, filling the continent once again. Melt water from residual mountaintop glaciers and snow cover feeds steady rivers which sustain a thriving ecosystem. Atlantis is flowering, population densities of plants and animals grow. With it, Neanderthal and Habilis population densities climb.

The Neanderthals have begun to work copper. Copper deposits are plentiful of on the tectonic uplift that is Atlantis. These deposits are carried down by the new post glacial streams, leaving rich caches of placer copper.

Formal trade networks evolve between Neanderthal communities as copper tools spread through the continent. Population density drives more sedentary lifestyles. Permanent or semi-permanent communities establish themselves near salmon and sturgeon spawning runs, monopolizing the harvests there, storing them for hard times and using the new practice of trade to extract goods from the excess harvest. Similar permanent or semi-permanent groups monopolize migration bottlenecks, eel grounds. Elsewhere the Neanderthal drift closer to agriculture, and to micro-livestock domestication.

The Ice Road has come to an end in the changed climate. It has evolved into the Volta do Mar, a circular current from Africa, to the Canaries, to Portugal. Further north, the Gulf stream pushes from the coast of Europe and England, up the coast of Atlantis and then to Scandinavia.

Mesolithic humans from ten thousand years ago onwards have begun to travel in dugout canoes. Boats swept up in the erratic post ice age currents are swept to Atlantis. Again, the mortality rate is high. There's a contribution of Mesolithic techniques which slowly filters through.

However, some of the Mesolithic humans survive as a culture. Whether escaped Neanderthal slaves, or castaways who have managed to find a refuge not dominated by Neanderthals, a human society begins to establish itself along the lower coastlines and southern fringes of Atlantis, dwelling in the swamps and marshes.

The Neolithic revolution, the invention of agriculture, begins in the middle east around twelve thousand years ago and begins to spread outwards, reaching the Atlantic coastlines of Europe around 7,000 years ago. Sometime between 6000 and 5000 years ago, the Neolithic farmers colonize Ireland.

It's around this time that a group of Neolithic dugout canoes are swept out into the current. This may have been a group from the English coast trying for Ireland, or perhaps wanderers along the French or Portuguese coasts. Certain forms of linguistic analysis suggests that these people were actually proto-Basques.

The group manages to survive by lashing their dugout canoes together for stability. Although currents are rough and the lashings are often torn, pairs and trios of canoes often hold together, maximizing stability, and the group reforms. A few canoes sink, the survivors being taken by other dugouts. All in all, two thirds of the group, thirty-eight individuals, including several women and children survive to reach the southern shores of Atlantis - the first time that an entire cultural community has made the trip.

On the southern shores, the survivors manage to establish themselves in the meadows and marshlands. They come from a grain based agricultural tradition, but seed stocks and tools have not survived the journey. The wild grasses and cereals of Atlantis' south are not particularly well suited for cultivation or domestication, and a starving group of survivors are not inclined to try to start from scratch. Instead, they focus on intensive harvest of wetland plants, including typha, also known as cattails or bullrushes.

Agriculture, however, is part of their cultural legacy. They adapt to their environment, farming and harvesting cattails as their new domesticate. Cattail roots are called rhizomes, and in season have a productivity greater than even wheat or potatoes, up to 32 dry tons per acre, or 6400 pounds of flour with a nutritional value of 266 calories per hundred grams.

The limitations Cattails were specialized marshland habitat, requiring a depth of shallow water to grow. In comparison, potatoes of wheat can be planted and harvested from any field. As with rice production in Asia, expanding cultivation required increasing investment in land and water management, including eventually water retention and drainage in large terraces or paddies.

The other downside is that cattail basins are eventually poisoned with cattail waste products and becomes useless - the marsh is then colonized by other species. This requires periodic field rotation - i.e., the cattail farmers have to establish new planting fields every few years.

The old fields are left back to nature, or used to cultivate other plants, or become habitats for frogs, beavers, and muskrat. A unique marshland agricultural complex emerges, one which owes an intellectual legacy or inspiration to the grain based agriculture of the mainland, but which is quite independent.

These Neolithic Atlantean humans become adept at local hydrological engineering - following the examples of beavers to build local haphazard dams, to raise and lower water levels, flood areas, divert streams. They move and fish among the streams and ponds in flat bottomed craft, pushing by poles.

They domesticate beaver and muskrat, even otter. They hunt crocodiles, and fear and worship the ultra-sized crocodilians that rule the southernmost reaches of Atlantis.

Gomphotheres or shovel tusked elephants are domesticated quickly. The animal's habitat overlaps, and they can be fed on cattails by product. They're water tolerant and provide a major source of draft animal horsepower. Although Elephants are normally long lived and slow growing, the Gomphotheres are smaller, about the size of cattle, and subject to predators, so they have evolved towards faster growth and reproduction. They fill a role equivalent to Water Buffalo in Asian cultures.

Their most remarkable accomplishment is rooted in their desperate campaign for survival on the voyage to Atlantis. They've discovered stability in lashing canoes together. This allows them to successfully fish and travel along the stormy Atlantic shorelines and survive the fierce waves. This eventually evolves into double hulled and outrigger canoes, an innovation not to be repeated until the Polynesians millennia later.

These new Atlanteans come to dominate the south and coastlines, their culture and lifestyle overwhelming or incorporating many of the Mesolithic human groups. Settled stable communities dot the south and coast. Something very like towns and even cities emerge.

But there's a flaw in the Atlantean agricultural package - it's not terribly portable. The situation is similar to the Agricultural complex of the ancient Ethiopians - it was an effective agricultural package, but it was suited only to the highlands of Ethiopia, and could not expand to the surrounding lowlands.

The Atlantean Agricultural package is suitable for marsh and wetlands, and even with extensive damming and stream diversions, there's limits to how far it can extend, or how many acres it can occupy. The Atlantean agricultural complex is confined to the southern lowlands, river basins, and coastal wetlands of the south and center. Beyond the Atlantean farmers are the fringe of Mesolithic barbarians, hunters and gatherers.

In these southern regions, land use varies strongly. Productive agricultural centers support immense population densities. But population densities drop dramatically away from centers of cultivation. The result is the emergence of dense population clusters, and early development of towns and cities. The need for systematic water regulation and the need to steadily build and maintain massive Earthworks resulted in high levels of social complexity and hierarchy.

Another shortcoming is that the nature of the Atlantean agricultural package meant that its culture and cultural centers are largely removed or distant from a number of key resources - Ivory is difficult to come by, flint even harder, copper all but impossible, hardwoods were inaccessible, furs, and so forth.

Three fourths of the continent is still the territory of the Neanderthals. They are simply too well established. But the Neanderthals have evolved an elaborate internal trade network. An intense trading relationship emerges between the emerging Neanderthal polities and the human communities.

The Neanderthals offer copper, ivory, large bones, even forest wood. The humans offer fine furs from beaver, otter and muskrat, crocodile hides, shellfish, beads and pearls. The exchange is mutually beneficial, with humans using copper and ivory to manufacture more elaborate and stronger tools, reinforcing their agriculture.

In addition to the domestication of the Gomphotheres, they acquire a secondary domesticate. Marsh agriculture is very labor intensive, and communities sometimes resort to slavery or forced labor. Captured Neanderthals make poor slaves, however. But the Atlantean humans find that Homo Habilis makes a very useful domesticate or slave for such labor, something Neanderthals are tolerant of and willing to help capture.

The intense exchange of goods results in language exchange and with it the flow of ideas. Neanderthals pick up the fundaments of agriculture, pushing their haphazard proto-agricultural practices into actual cultivation. The Neanderthals never fully adopt agriculture, but adopt widespread horticultural practices - garden plots everywhere. They are more systematic in the cultivation or raising of small domesticates. These new innovations, and the intensity of trading activities lead to areas of permanent population density - towns, regional polities.

All of this within a period of 5500 to 4500 years ago. The progression is not steady or even. Atlantis is subject to periodic earthquakes and volcanic eruptions, tsunamis sometimes wash sections of the shoreline. Both the Atlantean agriculturalists, the Monoliths, the Neanderthals and Habilis experience local and regional rises and falls, reverses and triumphs. And yet, progress marches forth.

Atlantis Ascending

Between 4500 and 3500 years, the fundaments of a Neolithic civilization grew up slowly on Atlantis. Cities and empires emerged, dynasties were fashioned. The Atlanteans built pyramids and monuments, temples and vast architecture. They learned to construct cities which were networks of canals instead of streets, often carefully spiraling waterways of near concentric circles, with elaborate channels and locks to ensure the flow of water, and to regulate the speed of flow. They learned to transport huge stone blocks, to dig into the mire to solid gravel or bedrock and then to build upward. They conceived elaborate rituals, prayed to strange gods.

A fundamental part of the Atlantean cultural tradition - or the human civilization of Atlantis - were the double hulled canoes with which the Atlanteans travelled and traded along the shores. The largest canoes were fifty feet long and could hold forty or more paddlers and cargo. Low sails helped to speed the boats along when the wind was favorable.

Unfortunately, the Atlantean boats tended to trade stability for maneuverability. They were often blown or taken further out by currents than intended, and the sailors would have to struggle back. The practice emerged of overprovisioning boats, to account for these events.

Sometime between 3700 and 3200 years ago, the Atlanteans had largely explored the coastlines of their Island continent. Towards the end of this period, they had become vaguely aware of Ireland and England. But these lands were already inhabited by alien peoples of unknown language and fierce disposition, and offered nothing to trade which appealed to the Atlanteans. There were a few attempts to establish outposts or colonies in suitably marshy areas. But on the whole the climate and landscape was unsuitable, and the prior inhabitants unwelcoming.

Starting 3200 years ago, over the next few hundred years, several Atlantean ships, mostly fishing or war expeditions, were caught up in the Volta Del Mar, and carried to the Portuguese shore. Eventually over this period, the Atlantean explorers learned to travel the Volta Del Mar circuit, to find their way back.

Much of the shorelines of Africa and Iberia was largely inhospitable to Atlantean agriculture - wild cattails grew everywhere, but the Atlantean domesticated varieties had more difficulty and were vulnerable to European plant and marsh diseases. Atlantean agriculture operated in the context of centuries of accumulated labor to build earthworks, ponds, water retention and drainage to maximize acreage whereas European cultivation was limited to the acreage that nature provided. Also problematic, it was difficult if not impossible to transport the Gomphotheres whose draft labor was essential to Atlantean agriculture. So this foreign landscape did not seem much more interesting than the largely worthless British Isles.

There was some encounters with the native populations, and some degree of trade particularly for copper and tin, which the Atlanteans valued highly for bronze, and knew only from the Neanderthals. But the distance and relative hardship made it too expensive to make extensive use of.

Civilization was Atlantis - the kingdoms of the south and the Neanderthals of the north. The barbarians beyond the sea had nothing that the Atlanteans could imagine wanting, and their land was inhospitable and unsatisfactory.

Nevertheless, roughly 3100 to 3000 years ago - by which time the currents and the shorelines around Europe were well understood, one Kadeth, an Atlantean prince, or perhaps a merchant, or perhaps an exile or merely a madman, resolved to establish a colony in the southern marshlands of the Iberian peninsula, in the vicinity of Tartessos.

The native Iberians possessed both copper and tin, and the hope was that a permanent city or at least a secure trading post might make the arduous sea journey cost effective. Copper, by this time, had become a previous and difficult commodity. Atlantean civilization had a perpetual shortage of copper due to the Neanderthal monopoly. Atlantean efforts to conquer and hold copper deposits had not turned out well.

The trading mission to the Iberian Tartesssans turned was successful, and a steady current of copper, tin and gold began to flow to Atlantis. The Atlanteans advanced to bronze working.

Sometime around 3000 years ago, sailors of Kadeth found their way through the straits of Gibraltar into what the Atlanteans called 'The Sea of Tranquility' - the Mediterranean. The Mediterranean was a momentous discovery. Unlike the Atlantic, which was stormy, treacherous and difficult, the Mediterranean, in comparison was almost placid. It could be sailed without difficulty or struggle, hospitable shores or islands were never far away.

Just as important, the climate was warm, humid, rivers flowed in everywhere with river deltas forming, marshes and swamps dotted the shores. Copper, gold and tin could be found. Ivory and elephants in the south. There were inhospitable regions, deserts in the south, but that could easily be bypassed. In many areas, the climate and landscape was an excellent match for the most productive heartlands of Atlantean civilization.

To the Atlantean kingdom, this was like a promised land - a sheltered and gentle sea whose shores were so hospitable, it seemed to have been made for them. It was made to be colonized, tailored to the needs and preferences of the Atlanteans.

The Atlantean Kingdom authorized a series of expeditions to explore the entirety of the Mediterranean - to discover its length and breadth, to learn the nature of the peoples who lived therein, to determine what wealth and trading opportunities presented and to find suitable locations for cities based around Atlantean agriculture.

Between 3000 and 2900 years ago, the great fleet of Namatos of Atlantis sailed to the Nile, and encountered the Egyptian civilization.

Discovery of the Inner Civilisations

The discovery of a series of powerful alien civilizations - the Egyptians, the Minoans, Phoenicians, Mycenaean's, came as a transformative shock to the Atlanteans.

In many ways, these civilizations were superior to the Atlanteans, a fact which may be apparent only in hindsight. On the one hand, the Atlanteans had managed to map the European and African coasts to an extent, had found and traversed the Mediterranean, and established themselves as the greatest explorers of antiquity. Their cities were large and populous, their economies, their mathematics and astronomy as complex.

On the other hand, the Atlanteans were still a Neolithic or stone age civilization, spending centuries hovering at the edge of the bronze age, perpetually starved for copper. The civilizations of the Eastern Mediterranean on the other hand were awash with metals - copper, gold, lead, silver and tin for the taking - they were fully bronze age societies, and the availability of bronze weapons and tools vastly extended their abilities.

The Atlanteans had their Gomphotheres, in comparison slow growing and slow breeding, as a labor domesticate - the Mediterranean civilizations sported horses, donkeys, cattle, sheep, goats, pigs, all faster breeding, faster growing, producing pound for pound more horsepower.

And the Mediterranean civilizations had cereal grains - wheat, barley, emmer, sorghum - crops for which their draft animals were well suited, and which were far more portable and flexible. They could be grown far more widely, in more areas, with less investment in building and maintaining landscaping.

Even at sea the Atlanteans were outmatched. Their ships, designed for stability in the savage Atlantic, were slow, small and unwieldy compared to the Mediterranean ships. The Mediterranean ships were designed for carrying large cargoes, or for war, across relatively short distances.

Ultimately, the mutual impression of each was of a strange, alien and immensely powerful civilization in the far distance.

Atlantis could not simply ignore the Mediterranean. Atlantis was a society starved of metals, on the cusp of the bronze age - Iberia offered the metals and the alien civilizations offered advanced secrets of bronze and metalworking. This, in and of itself, was transformative.

The Atlanteans also adopted most of the Mediterranean domesticates - horses and cattle were introduced to Atlantis, as were sheep and goats, pigs, cats and domesticated dogs. Rats were an unwelcome but inevitable guest. Grapes were adopted and incorporated readily into the Atlantean agricultural complex, as were dates, pears, pomegranates and olives. Many of the new imported domesticated plants had major effects, displacing or undermining existing Atlantean domesticates, and disrupting the careful balances which underlay Atlantean agriculture.

The Atlanteans also attempted to import and experiment with grain and cereal crops, though with poor success. Atlantean population and agriculture was too heavily engaged with its marshland environment. Rice would have grown there, but it wasn't part of the Mediterranean package. Instead, the Mediterranean cereals were dry land grains and ultimately, Atlantean society found itself unwilling to make a leap that would have literally involved abandoning and or relocating cities, new population centers, new power structures, new economies and societies. It would also open up new spheres of conflict with the Neanderthal polities and the human barbarians of the hinterland.

Atlanteans would eventually embrace grains, but within Atlantis the process would be slow, taking centuries. Even then, grain growing within Atlantis would be considered the vocation of barbarians and the vulgar, grain areas would be subject to excessive taxation, starved for infrastructure, and often attacked from all sides.

Despite distance and obstacles, there was for a time a small but lively luxury goods trade and cultural exchange between Atlantis and the Mediterranean civilizations which had major effects on Atlantean civilization. Not all of these effects were good. Wholesale import and adoption of Mediterranean domesticated plants and animals transformed the Atlantean economy and society. But they also wreaked ecological havoc.

Not only domesticated plants and animals impacted the Atlantean ecology. Wild animals of all sorts - from Lions and Rhinos, Wolves, Foxes and Rabbits were imported for pets, for games, for private zoos, some of which escaped and began to compete with or prey upon native species. Plants from all over the Mediterranean and European and African coasts were also imported for the gardens of the wealthy.

And then there were the parasites, the fleas, tapeworms, mosquitos, the fungus, bacteria and virus, returned in human, animal and plant hosts, wild and domesticated, whose effects were subtle, but often the most devastating. Introduced insect, fungus and plant disease spread quickly through the domesticated cattails and other food plants of the Atlanteans resulting at times in crop failure and famine. Malaria was introduced to the marshlands for the first time. Atlantis was awash in invasive species.

Nevertheless the new Bronze age, the new wealth of metals, the greater advantages and efficiencies of metal tools, the new draft animals and the horsepower they brought, the new domesticated plants and animals created an economic boom in the cities of Atlantis, periods of runaway prosperity and expansion. The Atlantean cities quarreled with each other, fought the Neanderthals. Delicately balanced economies and agricultural complexes were disrupted and spiraled into instability and even collapse. Boom was replaced with bust, population driven by new commodities outran its limits and famine followed.

None of this was overnight of course, but took place over a period of centuries. It was for this period, neither an unmitigated bad or a wholesale good, but a complex of effects and impacts which continually interacted and which produced changes, some desirable, some dreaded, but many unanticipated, which worked out over time.

As this took place, Atlantis strove to colonize the Mediterranean, declaring for itself to all and sundry, its possession and rights to the western half of the sea. It's dominion would extend from Cyrenaica on the shores of Africa, to the Italian peninsula in Europe.

At immense costs, the Atlanteans established a series of cities, outposts, way stations and trading posts along the Mediterranean and along the Atlantic shores of Europe, Africa and the British Isles. Some Atlantean expeditions even reached as far as Denmark where they traded for Baltic Amber. Many of these failed, the territories being unsuitable for the Atlantean agricultural package, and the Atlanteans themselves being able to fully adapt.

Nevertheless, several of these cities and outposts were successful in establishing a 'silk road' of stations that amounted to a sustainable trade route between Atlantis and the eastern Mediterranean. Even more critically, the Iberian cities and posts brought a wealth of metals and goods fueling the boom of the Atlantean bronze age.

There were also periods of conflict early on - particularly with the Mycenae. The vast distances and impenetrability of the Atlantic to Mediterranean ships meant that there was no danger to Atlantis itself. But Mycenaean raiders and pirates devastated Atlantean outposts. In turn, Atlantis would laboriously assemble gigantic fleets which would then crawl the length of the world. The sheer numbers of the fleet would guarantee naval superiority, but simple logistics guaranteed that land campaigns would never get very far or last very long.

Ultimately, imperial overstretch, extraordinary costs, civil strife and a continuing series of natural disasters between 2700 and 2800 years ago, brought an end to the Atlantean Empire. The Atlanteans gradually but inevitably lost control of the Mediterranean seas to the Greeks and Phoenicians. Atlantean sailors were eventually confined to the Atlantic waters, with Cadiz, Tangier, Tartessos and Carthage as trading partners.

The Atlantean cities within the Mediterranean became dependent on Greek or Phoenician traders and came under their political and economic influence, perpetually diminishing. The Atlantean agricultural complex, handicapped by a poor or absent labor domesticate, and limited in its ability to expand was simply drowned out by a surround proliferation of grain growers. Several Atlantean cities simply dwindled away to nothing while Greek or Phoenician populations grew and eventually replaced them - leaving nothing more than a few odd place names and quaint customs.

A major blow was the collapse of the Tartessan culture in Spain as a result of natural disasters. Although the Tartessan culture eventually recovered, before eventually vanishing, the Atlanteans did not. Their role was supplanted by the Phoenicians.

Meanwhile, a series of increasingly virulent plagues ravaged Atlantean population, devastating human, Neanderthal and Habilis respectively. This combined with natural disasters at homes, including a devastating series of earthquakes and tsunamis which destroyed many of the key cities of the south precipitated an Atlantean dark age.

Atlantis vanished from the Mediterranean and the pages of history. The Phoenician explorer Haplup Amaca 2300 years ago ventured into the Atlantic ocean sailing up as far as the British Isles and declared Atlantis lost and sunk beneath the waves..

The Dark Ages of Atlantis

Economic and ecological collapse lead to civil war and famine. Natural disasters followed one after the other, as plagues devastated the population and cities literally fell apart. Invasions and massacres of Neanderthals and barbarians, and both natural and manmade destruction of the elaborate system of canals and ponding finished off the collapsing civilization. Many of the cities were abandoned to the marshes and the seas, the destitute survivors of the culture devolved to a scattered village existence of poverty and internecine warfare.

Atlantis more or less vanished from the Ancient mind, existing as little more than an ancient story and oblique metaphor. There were still occasional references. The Greeks and Romans wrote of the land of Thule, or of Hyperborea, attributing fanciful descriptions. Plato incorporated it into a fairy tale. Some grains of truth suggested encounters with the Neanderthals of Barbarians of Atlantis.

The Roman Emperor Caligula entertained an Ambassador from Atlantis, but after a week or so had him flayed alive and then burned. There is no proof that the 'Ambassador' was really from Atlantis. In the third or fourth century, a Christian theologian made a reference to Atlantis as a land of the ungodly.

Within Atlantis itself, the sailing tradition came to an end and was slow to be revived. The Atlanteans reverted to hide or reed boats and stuck to coastal fishing. The double hull design was lost. Atlantean naval knowledge was lost. The Atlanteans never ventured to sea again as boldly or in such numbers. There was some evidence of occasional or continuing contacts with both England and Iberia.

Between 2800 and 1500 years ago, Atlantean civilization rose up again and then fell twice, neither time reaching the heights previously achieved. A wholesale population collapse seems to have occurred around CE 541 - which coincided with the Plague of Justinian, believed to have been carried by a missionary, and aborted a third rise of civilization.

The Atlantis Invasions

Atlantis next appears in the historical record beginning roughly 750 AD, during the period of Celtic migrations. The earliest Celtic migrations appear around the fifth or sixth century. However, the period following 750 AD was a period of large scale and systematic migration up until roughly 900. During this period, the Celts or Celtish monks sailed as far north as Iceland and the Faroe Islands. However, the largest share of migration was on the then thinly populated eastern coasts of Atlantis. There the Celts, with a sophisticated grain based agricultural package and metallurgical tradition, systematically pushed back the bronze age Neanderthals.

The Celtic invasions were accompanied by new waves of disease and parasites which decimated the Atlantean population once again. Celtic missionaries and priests declared the Neanderthals as creations of Satan without souls, and called for their extirpation.

They also sought to bring Christianity to the human Atlanteans of the south. Among the effects of this were the wholesale slaughter of the Habilis slaves/domesticates, and the destruction of many monuments and works of the previous Atlantean civilizations - the last great library of Atlantean books was burned and the Atlantean scripts were obliterated in favor of Latin. All that remains of Atlantean literary tradition are broken and defaced inscriptions.

Unfortunately, the loss of Habilis did no favors to the human Atlanteans of the south. Together with the decline of Gomphotheres, this had represented a net loss of available draft labor. The marsh agriculture had, because of loss of manpower, new parasites (including new varieties of leech and mosquito), ecological disruption and poorly controlled water flows, functioned erratically. Christian priests report several major famines over the next few centuries.

The Celtic settlers fared poorly. Their grain based agriculture, particularly their preferred species, was poorly suited to the relatively thin soils of western Atlantis. Stripping soil cover resulted in desiccation and erosion, after a few harvests the soil would be barren, and settlers would move onto new lands. Imported goats and sheep scoured the native vegetation. Deforestation, particularly cutting away tree and forest cover around streams and rivers caused water tables to drop, leading to flash floods which cut through and carried away soil For the first time, parts of Atlantis reverted to desert. The Celts simply moved further into the interior compounding the damage.

On the heels of the Celtic migrations came the Norse. From roughly 950 to 1150 was the era of Viking invasions. The Norsemen devastated England and Ireland, ravaged the coasts of France, Germany and Spain. They colonized as far west as Iceland, Greenland and Vinland, and as far east as the Volga river, sailing down all the way to the Black sea and Constantinople.

Atlantis was not spared. The Vikings raided up and down the coasts, devastating both the Celts in the west and the native Atlanteans in the south. The last remnants of Neanderthal civilization shattered as the Neanderthals were pushed deep into the interior, into a bare subsistence existence. Again, the Norse introduced foreign crops and foreign animals into new areas, settling heavily in the North and northern shores, and pushing the Celts south.

By 1200, the Atlanteans were confined entirely to marshlands in the south, a minority in their own homes.

In 1300, in a letter to the Pope, a Bishop assigned to the diocese wrote: "There has never been a more barren land, or more pathetic wretches. Here the proud Norse is worn and broken, the mighty Celt is destitute. To travel the land is to give witness to the meanest patches of scrub, dust everywhere blowing and abandoned farms land baked hard as clay. The meanest and most destitute by far or the people of the marsh, covered in filth, who wallow as the pigs."

It would get worse.

The Final Fall of Atlantis

In the 1400's, two further disasters befell Atlantis, one obvious, one subtle. The first was the delayed appearance of the black death - the bubonic plague.

The plague had torn through Europe in the 1300's, but it had taken time to vector its way into Atlantis, crawling first into Scandinavia, then infecting the Norse settlers of Atlantis, and then burning its way south, decimating the Celts, all but obliterating the Neanderthal and devastating the native Atlanteans and bringing about the final collapse of any remnants of higher Atlantean culture, and the final abandonment of the old Atlantean Agricultural package. Roughly half of the Norse and Celts and as much as 80% of the Neanderthals and Atlanteans died to the black death.

The other disaster, the subtle one, was Christopher Columbus discovery of the New World in 1492.

The Portuguese, had, of course rediscovered Atlantis earlier on, if in fact, it had ever been lost. Atlantis appears on Portuguese maps dating to the late 1300's, although fancifully rendered. But through much of the 1400's, Atlantis had been considered worthless. The people destitute, without minerals or appreciable natural resources, much of the land apparently unsuitable for farming. There were rumors of elephants in the interior, and occasionally a bit of ivory would show up. But Ivory could be had more cheaply from Africa. The truth was that there was nothing Atlantis had that anyone wanted. The Portuguese and Spanish were principally concerned with finding alternative routes to China and India. Atlantis wasn't even remotely on that route.

The discovery of the new world changed all that in significant ways. One of the key elements was the desperate need for manpower it produced. Christopher Columbus, and following him, the various Spanish conquistadors, set about enslaving the native population with a vengeance, extorting every ounce of gold and silver they could lay their hands on.

Thereafter, the West Indies became the focus of plantation efforts and a burgeoning sugar industry. In the relentless quest for more and more, entire populations were enslaved and obliterated. The Taino of the Caribbean were rapidly driven to extinction. As their population collapsed, the Spanish discovered a desperate and pressing need to replace that lost manpower.

They turned to Atlantis.

The papal decree by which the Neanderthals and Habilis had been determined to be 'made in the image of men, but not men, animals without souls, and mockeries by the hand of Satan' was now applied informally to all the inhabitants, nominally even the Norse and Celts. Although the Church objected, this became the de facto belief and practice of persons engaged in the Atlantis trade, even priests. Slavers and slave catchers roamed up and down the coasts of Atlantis. Celtic or Norse communities were bribed to sell each other out, a bounty was placed on heads and a leading occupation became slave hunting.

Innumerable numbers of Atlanteans of every origin were rounded up and sold, to a short life of being worked to death in the Caribbean.

In 1576, experimental Sugar plantations were established in the southernmost reaches of Atlantis. By this time Black slaves were being regularly taken. A few of these black slaves were brought to Atlantis, with the results of new waves of epidemics, although by this time, the Atlantean populations were so few and so scattered that it made little difference.

By 1594, slave raiders in a succession of six raids destroyed the last known villages of the original Atlanteans. The

Atlanteans as a culture were ended. A handful of individuals and families persisted.

In the 1600's, various European powers engaged in ventures. Tobacco was grown in the east, sugar in the south. The highland plains became home to hordes of sheep. Massive logging and deforestation took place. The desertification which had afflicted the eastern coasts became endemic through a large part of the country.

By 1690 the Neanderthals were believed to be extinct. In 1721 the last known Atlantean elephant herd was killed for ivory. Most, if not all of the Megafauna was extinct by the end of the 18th century. By the late 19th, the last old growth Atlantean forest cover had been logged, with the final stands being destroyed in wildfires as a result of droughts from the collapse of the water table.

In 1772 the last known pure blood Atlantean was brought to the Court of the Sun King as a 'guest' for exhibition, a gift from the Spanish King. He was dressed in what French courtiers imagined to be classical Atlantean garb, and often invited to speak in his native language. Transcriptions of these speeches indicate a large number of Celtic, Latin, Spanish and Scandinavian words, and much that appears to be simply gibberish, but there are also a number of recurrent combinations of phonemes to which he had inscribed meaning, that some believe may be actual Atlantean words.

He died in 1779. In 2005, the corpse was exhumed and DNA testing determined that he was in fact an authentic Atlantean. Examination of the historical record shows that the last verifiable previous, Atlantean had died in 1768.

And the story of Atlantis, my friends, is done.

The End

The Retroverse

An Accidental Cinematic Universe

Introduction

Cinematic Universes and Shared Universes are a big thing nowadays, mostly inspired by the thirty or so films of the Marvel Cinematic Universe.

We've seen the DC Cinematic Universe, the Dark Universe, DC Animated Universe, View Askew Cinematic Universe, and so on, along with the DC and Marvel Comics Universe. But these things go way back - Toho's Monster universe in the 60's and 70's, Universal Studios monster universe in the 30's and 40's.

Most of these fictional universes are more accumulated than designed. Someone tries something, a story, a book, a television show, a movie. It succeeds. They do something kind of similar, that does well. They keep doing it. After a while, it just makes sense to connect these overlapping properties and have a crossover, if that works, there are more. A kind of over-arching narrative emerges, and voila, you've got a shared universe. Marvel is more designed than most of them, but even there, that's basically it. It's almost never as thought out as you might expect. Mostly, they just evolve.

There is a Cinematic Universe out there, under our noses, overlooked and forgotten. Ladies and gentlemen, I give you...

THE RETROVERSE!

The Universe of 1950's and 1960's Science Fiction Movies.

Late one night, I was watching an old Sci Fi double bill - This Island Earth and Queen of Outer Space. If you haven't seen them, here are the plots: This Island Earth is set in the 1950's, human aliens who are all men with high foreheads come to Earth to trick a bunch of scientists into working for them, it seems that there is an interplanetary war, and they're losing badly. Queen of Outer Space is set in the 1980's, a spaceship from Earth is swept out to Venus, where they discover a women only civilization, it seems that in the recent past they had a war with a planet called Morda ruled by men. It was a battle of planets and sexes, and they won.

It was late at night, I was a bit fuzzy. So, I was watching it, and I thought.

"What if it was the same war?"

What if the war that the Metaluna were losing so badly in This Island Earth, was the same war that the Venerians had won in Queen of Outer Space? What if those movies were connected. What if it was the same universe?

But if they were connected, what else is connected? The matte paintings of the alien city in This Island Earth were re-used in Killers From Space. The Earthmen's uniforms from Queen of Outer Space are actually from Forbidden World. The spaceship set is from Flight to Mars. The spaceship footage is from World Without End. Eric Fleming who plays the lead Earth astronaut plays an identical role as an Earth astronaut on a mission to Mars in Conquest of Space. Laurie Mitchell who played the horribly scarred Queen Ylanna, of Venus' amazons, was also in Missile to the Moon about a race of lunar amazons, where she played the similarly named

Princess Lambda, whose romance with an Earthman results in her being face horribly. These two movies link to six other movies.

When you start looking, there's a lot of overlaps and connections.

The spacesuits built for Destination Moon went into the costumes warehouse, where they requisitioned or rented, and eventually showed up in sixteen different movies and television series. Stock footage of a German V2 rocket launch was used over and over again. Effects footage of spaceships got re-used. Even monster costumes got re-used.

Actors showed up over and over in identical roles - John Agar kept fighting aliens, Morris Ankrum played an army man, Marilyn Hanold and Laurie Mitchell played space Amazons.

Even when movies didn't share the same actors, or the same props, or the same special effects, there's weird symmetry, this recurrence of tropes:

Imagine aliens who are single eyed creatures at the center of fibrous nests of tentacles. That seems pretty unique. But that's the Trollenberg Terror, They Came From Outer Space, The Atomic Submarine, The Green Slime. Once would be interesting, two a coincidence. But the same peculiar type through four movies?

What about an alien world ruled by or made up almost exclusively of women? Or space travelling amazons come to Earth? Queen of Outer Space, Missile to the Moon, Cat Women on the Moon, Fire Maidens From Outer Space, Devil Girl From Mars, Frankenstein vs the Space Monster, Nude on the Moon, Abbot and Costello Go to Mars, Invasion of the Space Women, Voyage to the Planet of Prehistoric Women, Los Astronautas, Space Ship Sappy, Flying Saucer

Daffy, Invasion, the Astounding She Monster, Invasion of the Star Creatures, Ship of Monsters, Space Thing, Alien Women It shows up so often it's almost pathological

Then there are questions: Why in the movies set in the 1950's and 1960's, every time we turned around, aliens were invading? And it was different aliens every time, representing Mars, Venus, Galactic Federations, Planet X's. Sometimes they claimed to be from the same planet but had completely different motivations. We had so many alien invaders, they were practically stumbling over each other. It was like a freeway down here. We needed to put up traffic signs for all the visitors.

If they were all connected, why were they so contradictory - sometimes it was 'We are on a mission of peace!' Sometimes it was 'Kneel before Zod, puny humans!' Sometimes they were reanimating the dead. Sometimes they were blowing up rockets. Sometimes they were making people gigantic, or hiding out in caves stealing our cable, or trying to have sex with us. You just never knew.

And by the way, why were most of these invasions so puny, often one ship, a few crew, maybe some robots. You'd think if this was an interstellar or interplanetary civilization, they'd just squash us flat - send the space battleship and game over. And there are a couple of big movies where that's sort of tried - War of the Worlds and Earth vs the Flying Saucers. But mostly, the average invasion force seemed to consist of one saucer, a bickering couple and their pet monster? I'm sorry? Their world is invading ours, and that was the best they could? If you watch enough of these movies put together, it feels like we're the victims of passive aggression from outer space.

But then, the weird thing is, when you watch the movies set in the future, it's like we encounter a completely different set of aliens. Where did all the invaders go? Where are all the ones who were invading us, or visiting with important messages? Instead, we just get the cosmic equivalent of the Swedish Bikini Team, and a lot of innocent looks and shrugs.

What exactly is going on out there in outer space? I've talked about connecting these movies, but there are as many contradictions as congruencies.

Aesthetically and thematically, these movies presented a unified vision of what the future looked like, inspired by Chesley Bonestell artwork, a vision of spaceships like silver needles with tail fins and cratered alien landscapes. It was a vision where aliens flew in flying saucers and women ruled in outer space. The practicalities of World War II industrial war production, and lurid artistic visions of pulp magazines fused together, giving a remarkably uniform visual sensibility and production design. Added to that was a visual documentary style that merged newsreels with conventional movies. Even when they weren't borrowing each other's props and costumes, these movies tended to look like each other. The vision of the future, or even of the sci fi present, was remarkably consistent.

The same ideas percolate through these movies - alien invasions, space travel, giant monsters, atomic war, mixing and matching, weaving in and out. They reflected the sensibilities and attitudes of the time. Russia and Communism is barely mentioned, but there's a recurring theme of subversion, of being infiltrated, of being taken over. A lot of movies can be read as metaphors for cold war issues. Sexual politics are in full effect, but often confused, and subtly challenged. Sometimes it's deliberate, quite often it's just the ideas and attitudes floating around expressing themselves.

These movies came from a distinctive era, a kind of unheard of social consensus. This was the post-war era, where

America had thrown off the depression and gone on to singlehandedly defeat both Nazi Germany and Imperial Japan, while containing the Soviet menace. It was a time where technology was progressing by leaps and bounds, literally from biplanes to fighter jets, to supersonic aircraft. During this period, space travel went from an impossible dream, to the first satellites, manned rockets, a Russian space station and American moon landings.

If you watch enough of these movies, if you start looking for connections - thematic, tropetastic, recurring actors/roles, props, stock footage, costumes you can find an underlying architecture - an entire alternate universe and history that hangs together.

Five Million Miles From Earth

Unravelling the Retroverse involves a bit of detective work. The Retroverse, all the movies that constitute the cinematic universe are like snapshots of parts of the big picture. Some of the snapshots are large, some are small, but none of them are the complete picture. The picture is what emerges from the connections.

For instance - In 2001: A Space Odyssey, mysterious unseen aliens come to Earth millions of years ago and uplift apes into humans, leaving automated installations on the Moon and around Jupiter. Five Million Years to Earth, gives us insect-like aliens came to Earth millions of years ago, uplifted apes into humans, and buried its own controls and coding in humanity. It doesn't really make sense that two different races of aliens would come by millions of years ago and separately uplift humans. So... same aliens? Which means the 2001 unseen aliens were insectoids.

But then in the First Men in the Moon, and Melies much earlier Trip to the Moon, we see insectoid aliens in small colonies on the moon. The moon is a dead and lifeless world, and always has been. Anything or anybody living there came from somewhere else. So are the Insectoids in these movies the degenerated remnants of the race from Five Million Years to Earth? We know that the 2001 aliens were active on the moon.

Both 2001 and Five Million Years featured an incredible technological civilization and powerful psychic machines, some of which resemble black monoliths, which can manipulate minds and matter even today. But with the exception of a few small degraded remnants on the moon, they're not around physically - they don't show up overtly in the rest of the Retroverse. So they're extinct?

Forbidden World is set on an alien planet where the original race, the Krell, is now extinct. We don't know what they looked like, but they're clearly non-human. But they have incredibly powerful psychic machinery which is still active millions of years later, as in 2001 or Five Million Years. Oddly, the Forbidden World features Earth animals and vegetation, including tigers. How do tigers end up on an alien world, humanity didn't bring them. The implication is that the extinct Krell must have visited Earth millions of years ago and transplanted Earth life to their world.

This creates a piece of the picture for us, the deep history of the Retroverse. Millions of years ago, a race of insect like aliens, the Krell arose. They developed interstellar travel and powerful psychic machines. They travelled the universe, finding Earth, where they manipulated apes, evolving them into humans. The Krell civilization collapses for unknown reasons. Although their apparently becomes physically extinct on their home world, their machineries continue to operate. Relic populations survive in their lunar outposts until the late

19th century, having regressed to a primitive state. Eventually, in the future, humanity rediscovers their world, and names them as the Krell.

Rise of the Psychic Monsters

The Krell may not have gone completely extinct, stick with me here. They're definitely not around much in physical form. As noted, there are only a couple of movies which feature Insect-humanoids.

But in Planet of the Vampires, space travelers visit a dead world inhabited by bodiless creatures of psychic energy. These creatures are able to occupy and animate dead bodies, or even temporarily possess living humans, they explain that they were once physical beings but 'upgraded.' That turned out to be a mistake, so they want off their dead world, and they need bodies and spaceships to do it. The big twist is that the human space travelers are aliens themselves, before the psychic monsters take over, they cripple their spaceship so that it can't reach their world. The psychic monsters are forced to head for the closest planet: Modern day earth.

They Came From Outer Space features psychic monsters coming to Earth in a meteor shower (or possibly the fragments of a damaged spaceship breaking up in the atmosphere?), and proceeding to take possess humans, reanimate the dead, and start building rockets to go to the moon. They explain that they once had physical bodies, but upgraded, a decision they now regret. They were tooling around in a spaceship, but things went wrong.

It's not really that hard to draw a line from Planet of the Vampires to They Came From Outer Space, and even back to Forbidden World and the Krell. After all, the Krell created powerful psychic machines, and the movie suggests that they were destroyed by their own psychic creations.

There is a hole in the story. Of course, there's little evidence of the psychic monsters on Forbidden World like the ones in Planet of the Vampires. But perhaps, as they were being destroyed by their creations, the Krell managed to cleanse their world leaving only remnants in space. Or their creations fled the planet and were trapped in space or on outer worlds.

There are other, instances of bodiless aliens reanimating corpses, notably Invisible Invaders and Cape Canaveral Monsters.

Let's think about it for a moment. What would it be like to be a bodiless psychic being, a creature of energy, unable to touch or affect the material world directly, except by possessing a host... and there are no hosts around.

What would it be like to spend thousands, maybe even millions of years in that state? People get squirrely if cramped up alone for a couple of weeks? Many of these psychic monsters would probably opt to end themselves. Some would hold it together, with some forming communities and working together, others operating alone. Some would go insane. Some would regress to brutal animalistic states, hungry only to occupy a body, any kind of body - like corpses in Night of the Living Dead, severed arm in the Crawling Hand, or even a crude machine such as the Killdozer.

Space Atlantis and the Matriarchy

Sometimes when you are putting a puzzle together, you get a missing piece. You don't know what that piece is, or what's in that piece. But you can tell it's there from the other pieces around it. You can even figure out what shape it is, and what's in the missing piece.

We know the deep history of the Retroverse, the rise and fall of the Krell, their creation of humanity, their destruction at the hands of psychic monsters that they created.

But there's more history. For instance, in so many of these movies, when astronauts go out into space, they find people. They find people on the Moon in Cat Women on the Moon, Missile to the Moon, Twelve to the Moon; on Venus in Queen of Outer Space, Masters of Venus, Planet of Prehistoric Women; on Mars in Flight to the Mars, Rocketship X-M; around Saturn in Fire Maidens From Outer Space; and among the Asteroids in Phantom Planet.

In some cases, we find that these aliens are capable of and very much in favor of breeding with humans. Even a bit too enthusiastic: Mars Needs Women, Devil Girl From Mars, Frankenstein vs the Space Monster, Space Thing, Alien Women.

Well, stop and think. If it looks just like an earth human, walks like an earth human, talks like an Earth human, breathes the same kind of air, eats the same kind of food, lip-locks like an Earth human, and wants to make babies with Earth humans... Then they all have to be earth originally.

Did the Krell seed them all over the solar system? Doesn't seem likely, the time line is wrong. There isn't any evidence of other aliens in deep history.

So, if humans are all over the solar system, the logical conclusion is there must have been at least one previous civilization on Earth, before recorded history, that made it into space and established all these colonies. Call this Atlantis, the characters in the movies sometimes do. But this is not the classical Atlantis we think about, but an advanced, spacefaring high-tech Atlantis.

In fact, in some cases, the aliens trace their ancestry directly to Atlantis. The Fire Maidens From Outer Space, and the Masters of Venus both claim to be from Atlantis. In Warlords from Atlantis, the Atlanteans claim to be Martians who moved to Earth.

Mysteries of Atlantis and Space

So let's assume that most of the aliens in the Retroverse, the ones that look human at least, are actually descended from earth humans, they're from Ancient Atlantis, what can we tell about this Atlantis?

First thing - they're not around any more. So obviously, something happened to them. Stick a pin in that one.

Second - it was a powerful civilization. It spread through the solar system and beyond, and established a multitude of colonies which have lasted into the present era. That's engineering built to ten thousand year standards and beyond.

Through several movies, Wizards of Mars, Rocketship X-M, Angry Red Planet and Robinson Crusoe on Mars, we see that Mars has a (barely) breathable atmosphere, not quite enough to sustain life for long, but thick enough for animals, plants and for liquid water. That's definitely not our Mars. Terraformed or partly terraformed? Again, that's a powerful civilization.

There are a lot of space-societies that are literally women only, either totally female, or with only a tiny population of men: Queen of Outer Space, Missile to the Moon, Cat Women on the Moon, Fire Maidens From Outer Space,

Abbot and Costello Go to Mars, Voyage to the Planet of Prehistoric Women, Space Ship Sappy and more.

There are a lot of other societies where women are dominant, they're the official rulers, they are the ones captaining or piloting flying saucers, clearly making decisions in their cultures: Invasion of the Space Women, Los Astronautas, Flying Saucer Daffy, Invasion, Astounding She Monster, Invasion of the Star Creatures, Ship of Monsters, Space Thing, Alien Women and more.

Of course, not all of the societies out there are female or female dominated. But preponderance suggests that Atlantis was originally a matriarchal or amazon civilization, one where women rather than men ruled.

They mastered human longevity - on some of these colonies, the inhabitants appear to be hundreds, even thousands of years old, notably Fire Maidens from Outer Space and Abbot and Costello Go to Mars.

Several appear to show psychic abilities, hypnosis, telepathy, forms of telekinesis, but this is far from universal. Still, this does suggest a connection to the Krell, and may imply that Atlantis was able to advance quickly because they discovered or rediscovered Krell technology. Psychic powers show up in Abbot and Costello Go to Mars, Nude on the Moon and Cat Women on the Moon.

They also learned to create mutants, including humanoid mutants with expanded brains, disembodied brains and other creatures. Examples: This Island Earth, Ship of Monsters, Invaders from Mars, It Conquered the World and Zontar the Thing From Venus.

They created humanoid and ambulatory plants as guards, soldiers and workers. Even after the matriarchy fell, some of these plant monsters persisted. Some regressing to tree-like forms on a subarctic Island, another was frozen in ice until it was revived in the modern era. Others were used as guards or agents - Navy vs the Night Monsters, Invasion of the Saucer Men, The Thing From Another World and Invasion of the Star Creatures.

The Battle Beyond Earth's Sky

The preponderance of all these human societies on the Moon, Mars, Venus and elsewhere tells us that once about a time, there a major civilization, Atlantis, and it fell thousands of years ago.

So what happened after that? Here on Earth, civilization started over from the ground up and built itself back up. Mostly this is the history that we know, with a few wrinkles here and there.

But what happened out there?

By and large, very little. We know from the fact that many lasted to this day that they were self-contained and very well engineered. Build a habitat that lasts ten thousand years or so is top notch stuff. They were all designed to be self-sustaining and self-contained. So they didn't need anything from each other, and largely, they didn't have anything to offer to each other.

At the same time, these societies, individually or collectively lacked the resources to rebuild. We know that because they didn't. They didn't sweep back from outer space to rebuild Atlantean's civilization on Earth. They didn't build new colonies create a new civilization beyond the stars. They were built good enough to survive, but not to grow. So the only real option was splendid isolation.

Isolation also allowed the colonies to evolve in different directions socially. One society on Venus reverted to primitive savagery, in Planet of the Prehistoric Women. Other societies opted for gender equality, or even male domination, as in Masters of Venus, Plan Nine From Outer Space and This Island Earth.

Over time, things would occur. Some of the colonies probably failed, leaving only ruins behind. In Catwomen on the Moon, the colony is failing and the air is running out. That's why the 'cat women' are so desperate to escape to Earth. In Have Rocket will Travel, the heroes find an empty city on Venus, killed off by the cities master computer.

In other cases inbreeding and a small mutation spreading through the community might result in a colony diverging considerably from the human norm. They might start to have green skin or antenna, or in the case of one group of Martians, end up looking like scrawny Frankenstein monsters in Three Stooges in Orbit, or like goblins in Wizards of Mars and Space Monster. However, technology and incredibly long life spans probably guarded against that.

In at least some colonies there appears to have been reproductive dysfunction, with either loss of males, Devil Girl From Mars, or loss of females, Mars Needs Women and Frankenstein versus the Space Monster, or widespread sterility. In at least some of these cases though, the cause was war.

Which brings us to war. We've talked about This Island Earth and Queen of Outer Space, but they aren't the only movies that mention a war between worlds. In Devil Girl From Mars, a Martian dominatrix comes to Earth when her flying saucer breaks down, so she and her killer robot harass patrons of a local bar. She threatens them with her "perpetual motion ray." But mainly she's interested in a little heterosexual action.

It turns out that while no one on Earth was paying attention, her people had a gender based space war, and all the men got wiped out. So she needs replacements. Of course, the British don't go for that sort of thing at all so eventually one of them blows up her ship real good. She should have threatened to spank them all very severely.

Meanwhile, in Frankenstein vs the Space Monster, Princess Markuzan, who apparently shops at the same fetish store as the Devil Girl, is coming to Earth to abduct women, also because of a gender based space war. Markuzan is played by Marilyn Hanold, by the way, who also starred as a space amazon from Venus, in the Three Stooges short Space Ship Sappy.

That actually happened a lot in these movies by the way, in addition to Laurie Mitchell who played a space princess in Missile to the Moon who gets face eaten by a spider, and a face scarred ruler in Queen of Outer Space, there are also: Tania Velia and Mary Ford show up on Venus as amazons in both Missile to the Moon and Queen of Outer Space, Renate Hoy showed up as an amazon in Missile to the Moon and on Venus as well in Abbot and Costello Go to Mars, Nina Bara (Alpha) in Missile to the Moon and also as amazon Princess Tonga in Space Patrol. It's just one of those things.

But I digress.

So what's happening out in space is that over time a schism develops among the lost colonies of the Atlantis Matriarchy. While many or most remain female dominant, a minority evolve to egalitarianism or male domination. Perhaps coalitions begin to form. This minority calls themselves the Metaluna. War breaks out, the battle of the sexes is on. And the Metaluna are losing....

The War Above Comes to Earth

Anyone remember the Great War? Also known as World War One? How about World War II? Anyway, both times, it came down to Germany and France facing off against each other. Millions of troops on either side, fortifications and defenses up the wazoo. Stalemate, neither side could win.

Until, the Germans figured out a way to beat France.

They invaded Belgium.

Belgium was this small out of the way country known for chocolate and sprouts, and for being the underachieving version of the Netherlands, or sometimes France-lite. Historically, the Belgians have been invaded by the Celts, the Romans, the Goths, the Franks, the French, the Germans, the British, the Dutch, the Danes, the Norwegians, the Spanish, the Germans again, the Americans, etc.. So apparently no one likes them, so I guess it serves them right for standing around in the middle of two world wars, you knew someone was going to do it.

But by invading Belgium, the Germans could bypass all of France's defenses and fortifications and strike at Paris. It was a good strategy, it almost worked in WWI, and worked like a charm in WWII.

Earth was Belgium.

The reality was that the space people never really cared about Earth. It had 99% of the human population, and a planet full of resources. But on the other hand it was filthy, disease ridden, smelly, backwards and full of crude male dominated societies that thought beating each other with pointed sticks was the height of technology. The people there were barely human as far as the colonies were concerned. Once in a while a tourist might buzz the locals in a flying saucer, but that was about it. Nobody cared.

Except that the Metaluna were losing. They needed to pull a Belgium to survive, make a Hail Mary pass, do an end run, fight outside of the box.

So suddenly, the Metaluna got interested in Earth. Sure, smelly and primitive, but on the other hand, they'd invented flush toilets recently, radio, the combustion engine, the atomic bomb, rockets, they were making great strides, they had the beginnings of a crude industrial and manufacturing base.

The Metaluna were under pressure and short on everything. Taking over Earth could be a game changer. They would have access to Earth's vast stores of radioactive elements and mineral resources, Earth's power plants, it's industrial base which could potentially be upgraded. They could access Earth's greatest scientific minds, and perhaps with proper education, they could become useful. The Metaluna were losing and Earth offered a way to win.

And worse come to worse, if the Metaluna lost, they might need a new planet to live on.

Conquer Earth! Totally great idea. No downsides whatsoever.

Just one problem. All of the post-Atlantis colonies are small, they lack industrial bases. They're tooling around with flying saucers that are thousands of years old. Some of them so poorly maintained that they're leaking radiation and have to be flown wearing shielded suits in Earth vs the Flying Saucers.

To make matters worse, they fighting a defensive war, it's not as if they have a whole lot of resources to spare. In the middle of Plan Nine From Outer Space, the invasion force gets cut back from three whole saucers, to one, with one guy and a henchwoman.

While we're on the subject of Plan Nine from Outer Space, when you think about it, that means that they must have been at this for a while, if they'd already gone through eight previous plans. So what were the other eight plans? Looking at the movies, we can guess.

Nine Plans from Outer Space

Plan 1 - Reconnaissance and Information Gathering: By the 1950's, the Metaluna's knowledge came from a very limited spectrum of radio and television, and actually travelling down to Earth to learn the ways of the locals. Think of it as 'The Idiot's Guide to Conquering Earth.' This might lead to fairly innocuous encounters, Visit to a Strange Planet, a Martian in Paris. Or more dire operations such as kidnapping humans as in Thin Air, Not of This World, Cape Canaveral Monsters, Night Caller from Outer Space. Or field exercises in copying The Human Duplicators or Invasion of the Body Snatchers.

Plan 2 - Disinformation: as primitive as the Earth people are, they're coming along really fast and throwing atom bombs around, and there are a terrible lot of Earth people. Straight up conquest isn't really viable. So just flying in with a fleet of saucers and squashing them, not really much of an option. Another bad idea? Telling the truth to Earthlings probably wasn't a good option, they were a warlike, arrogant, difficult bunch. You probably didn't want the United States to know that you were few thousands or tens of thousands of people on ancient colonies left over from a fallen civilization tooling around on thousand year old flying saucers. Big awesome mighty spacemen with godlike supernatural powers was the way to go. It's like those old colonial stories where the

European explorers come to the African or Asian village and pass themselves off as demigods with supernatural powers After all, Earthlings were also a cowardly and superstitious lot, so all they needed to do was dress up like bats... Wait, wrong comic! But you get the point: Never tell the truth, claim to be from Mars or some other planet, make up a planet, claim to be from a dying world, exaggerate, mislead, use biological robots, baffle them with bullshit... In Devil Girl From Mars, the devil girl threatens the locals with her 'perpetual motion ray'? What does that even mean? ... The point is that disinformation was part of every operation.

Plan 3 - Peaceful Contact and Pacification, aka We come in Peace: Send an emissary, claim to be from some Galactic Federation, tell the rubes you come in peace, lecture them on their warlike ways, and try and get them to roll over. This actually describes the Flying Saucer contactee movement of the 1950's. Basically, back then, what would happen is that some random person would be walking along and a flying saucer would land in front of them. Some Nordic blondes would then come out, they'd offer the random person a joyride in their saucer, they'd say things like 'nice planet' don't screw it up, mention that nuclear war and environment degradation was bad. Sometimes they'd offer muffins (I'm not kidding). The most famous contactee was George Adamski. In terms of the Retroverse, the most famous visitor was Klaatu and his big robot Gort, in The Day the Earth Stood Still, but there were a handful of movies in this vein, The Cosmic Man, Rocket Man, Red Planet Mars. Variations included coming to peacefully ask for help for their dying world, as in The Man From Planet X, or just messing benignly with people. Typically, the effort to peacefully take over by pulling the wool over our eyes didn't go well, probably because of our stupid stupid minds. Sometimes the

Metaluna would start off 'we come in peace' and then get nasty, as in Santos vs the Martian Invaders.

Plan 4 - Covert Cells and Subversion: Classic spy stuff - set up an operation on Earth. Earth accomplices are enlisted in It Conquered the World and Zontar, the Thing From Venus. A criminal gang is enlisted in The Flying Disk Man of Mars. This Island Earth was a covert operation to enlist a bunch of Earth scientists to work on their problems. Three Stooges in Orbit features an alien effort to steal an inventor's military technology. The Flight That Disappeared seems to be about stealing scientists. Killers from Space tapped into America's power grid.

Plan 5 - Takeover by Mind Control and Possession: So the Earthlings don't want to do what you say. Simplest way to conquer them? Take over the leaders. Admittedly, a bit of practice was required to make sure you've got it right. So first take over some low level humans in out of the way spots and refine the techniques, try a few different approaches. It Came From Outer Space, Invaders from Mars, Quatermass II, They Came From Outer Space, It Conquered the World, Zontar, the Thing From Venus, The Brain From Planet Arous, Space Children, The Bubble, No Survivors, Not of This Earth. It's a terrific plan, they kept trying and trying. They just never quite got it right.

Plan 6 - Replacement with Doppelgangers: Mind control can be a bit iffy. Why not just replace Earthlings entirely. This was the entire plot of the 60's Sci Fi TV series, The Invaders, it's also I Married a Monster From Outer Space, The Human Duplicators, Invasion of the Body Snatchers, The Day Mars Invaded Earth. The only downside was that the doppelgangers were often clumsy and obvious. Again, they never quite got it right.

Plan 7 - Destabilization, Disasters and Giant Monsters: What would make a takeover of Earth nations easier? Throw a few disasters their way. That way, if they're off balance and running around coping, they won't notice if you take over or replace a few leaders here and there. Even better, you can show up and 'rescue' the Earthlings and take over while they're busy being grateful. For some reason, this seemed to translate to using giant creatures. This was actually part of the plan in both Robot Monster and Killers from Space, they were going to unleash giant lizards on human civilization. An alien is directly responsible for the Fifty Foot Woman. Monsters are unleashed in Teenagers From Outer Space, The Creeping Terror and Invasion of the Animal People. In The Strange World of Planet X, aliens 'coincidentally' intervene to rescue humanity from super-sized insects. Back in the 1950's, there were a lot of giant monster incursions - giant ants in Them, giant grasshoppers in The Beginning of the End, giant scorpions in The Black Scorpion, The Giant Mantis, Tarantula, The Giant Claw, The Beast from 20,000 Fathoms, etc. They always followed a pattern - these creatures would show up out of nowhere, mature and full size, often in large numbers, and then they'd start on an almost military campaign through small towns before heading straight to a large center... almost as if they were being arranged and directed, by some mysterious agency behind the scenes. What happened here? Mainly, Earth humanity was a bit too good at blowing things up.

Plan 8 - Invasion: This whole conquest of Earth thing was just not going well. The various plans were not well coordinated, and different plans kept moving ahead at different times in different locations. Information gathering was flawed, Earthlings were too suspicious when you were nice to them, too stubborn when you took over their minds, replacing them with doppelgangers never quite worked right,

and they kept blowing up the giant animals. A perfect strategy
to quietly take over Earth had turned into a shambles of
competing, under-resourced schemes getting in each other's
way. Meanwhile, the war with Venus was going from bad to
worse. The Metaluna were getting desperate. Even if they
weren't ready, it was time for the full scale invasion.... As seen
in Santos vs the Martian Invasion, Earth Dies Screaming, The
Day Mars Invaded Earth, and particularly, the big push Earth
vs the Flying Saucers. In the end, this too fails, the Metaluna
simply don't have enough ships to carry it off, the grand
strategy is a mess, the humans are too tough and Venus is
about to win its war and destroy Metaluna.

Plan 9 - Reanimation of the Dead aka They're Out of Ideas:
Seriously, this got dumped to the bottom of the list because it
was a bad idea, but someone importants' nephew proposed it
and no one could outright say no. Plan Nine From Outer
Space, Invisible Invaders, Night of the Living Dead. If
they've gotten this far down the list, they've pretty much lost
hope.

What's Love Got to Do With It?

While the Metaluna are desperately trying to take over Earth
in the vain hope of saving their bacon, what are the Venerians
doing? Mostly they're winning their war.

They don't really care about Earth. It's full of smelly,
primitive misogynists, and they're happy enough to let the
Metaluna flounder. Now and then, as in Flying Saucer Daffy,
or Invasion of the Star Creatures, they might buzz around to
see what the Earthlings are up to. But really, not a priority.

But after the war, the Venerians start to get a little concerned
about Earth. Earthlings are fine, on Earth. They're welcome
to it, it's a giant toilet. They can have it, good for them.

Earthling's in space? That's a lot less appealing. They might be wanting to put a stop to that.

And in fact, the early space program runs into a lot of obstacles. Such as a mysterious layer of wildly growing spores in Earth's upper atmosphere, so that anything that goes up comes back down contaminated, as we see in Space Master X7, The First Man Into Space, The Quatermass Xperiment, The Blob, Agent From H.A.R.M., and The Flame Barrier.

Female aliens attempt to obstruct the space program in Frankenstein Meets the Space Monster, Moon Pilot, Unearthly Stranger, Alien Women. There are other attacks on the space program by unidentified forces.

A series of asteroids move into a collision orbit with Earth, in Death From Outer Space and When Worlds Collide, some of them contaminated with mysterious spores in the Green Slime and The War Between the Planets - Earth is literally in a shooting gallery.

The Wars of All the Worlds

The universe of the Retroverse is largely a history of ancient alien relics and ruins, and small human civilizations scattered in pockets around the solar system with their robots and biological constructs. It's a history of a war between genders and worlds, happening above our heads, that we are barely aware of, and confused, poorly planned and equipped missions to Earth whose only real successes are deception and confusion. By and large that accounts for most of it.

There is one big anomaly. A genuine alien civilization, not human men, not human women, not insects or psychic constructs, mechanical or biological robots, but true genuine honest to god aliens, who appear in sufficient numbers and with sufficient power to squash humanity like a bug. That's the 'Martian' invaders of War of the Worlds.

The Enemy.

You were wondering what happened to the Matriarchy of Atlantis?

We find out in the Terrornauts. In this extremely low budget British production, an astronomer intercepts mysterious signals from the outer edges of the solar system. He makes contact with an automated installation and discovers that over ten thousand year ago, there was a star travelling civilization. It encountered another race they know only as the Enemy - a race of cold intelligences from smaller, colder worlds with tri-lobed ships using beam weapons, and implacable hostility. In the war that ensued, the Enemy were beaten back, but only at the cost of the fall of the civilization as the Enemy found a way to regress humans to savagery. But before it fell, it managed to construct a semi-automated defense installation, in case the Enemy ever came back. This installation requires humans, particularly a woman, to operate its weapons (apparently that requires wearing shower caps). And the Enemy are coming back.

The tri-lobed ships of the Enemy aren't quite the 'Martian' war machines of War of the Worlds, but there's a passing similarity. The fact that they come from 'smaller colder worlds' is also suggestive.

The time frame in the Terrornauts, the fact that the installation was built to protect the solar system, and the fact that it requires a woman to be fully operational all seem to point towards the Matriarchy of Atlantis. So now we know what happened to them, why the matriarchy fell, why Earth was reduced to savagery, and why the colonies were left on the vine. It also means that the events of Terrornauts were the first battle in the new War of the Worlds when that Enemy returned finally.

Robinson Crusoe on Mars, a manned mission goes wrong, leaving our hero as a castaway. Luckily he learns to survive, and even meets a 'Friday,' but from time to time, they're hunted by the war machines from War of the Worlds, which are established to be from deep space. Friday's word for the war machines? It's the same as in Terrornauts: The Enemy.

The new War of the Worlds wasn't confined to Earth alone. Robinson Crusoe explicitly establishes that the Enemy had invaded Mars, just as they did Earth. In fact Mars shows signs of the Enemy in other films. Angry Red Planet gives us a glimpse of a three eyed giant. Rocketship X-M features a ruined Martian city so recently destroyed that it is still radioactive, with the inhabitants reduced to savagery. Ruined cities show up in Angry Red Planet and Wizard of Mars. Like Robinson Crusoe, the Wizard of Mars, Rocketship X-M, Conquest of Space, Flight to Mars all feature crash landings. Mission Mars and Angry Red Planet features astronauts meeting a mysterious force hostile to their presence. Clearly Mars was attacked and devastated, generations later, they are still hostile to outsiders.

Although there's no evidence one way or the other, it's likely that the Enemy attacked the matriarchy colonies on Venus as well. If so, then the Venerians, after ten thousand years of relative peace, suddenly within a generation, have fought two savage wars, one against the patriarchy of Metaluna, and another against the old Matriarchy's nemesis, the Enemy. Do they really want to risk another interplanetary war, this one against the thuggish primitive patriarchies of Earth? Perhaps this is one of the reasons why, in the era of space travel there is so much early opposition and hostility to Earth going into space.

War of the Worlds is the War and Peace of the Retroverse, it is the great era spanning epic. This is not only the one true massive alien invasion, with clearly genuine aliens, it also connects us to many other films. . Byron Haskins, the effects director, went on to helm Robinson Crusoe, which is why the Martian war machines are identical in both movies. While it doesn't recycle costumes, sets or props from other movies, as was so common in this era, actors in War of the Worlds appeared as other characters in 37 other sci fi movies of the Retroverse. And it's loosely linked to other movies, most critically the Terrornauts. It may have been even vaster than we knew on Earth.

Here's a final speculation about the Enemy and the War of the Worlds. In the end, the Enemy were destroyed, not by anything Earthlings could do, but by simple bacteria. So the human race got lucky. Or did it?

Given how utterly alien the Enemy were, what are the odds they'd be affected by any earthly bacteria. Maybe it wasn't luck. Maybe the bacteria had been designed and seeded into Earth's atmosphere by the ancient matriarchy long ago, or by the Venerians as their contribution to the war. Food for thought.

Onwards to the Future...

There's more to the story of course. More details, more nuance. There's all these background connections between the movies, shared spaceships and stock footage, shared props and costumes, actors in the same roles, similarities in themes and stories. Some of them in quite surprising places. There's cheesy stories to dissect, background information to match up.

There are overlooked chapters: Lost matriarchy relics on Earth. An earlier history of space travel using cannons to reach outer space. Monsters to explain. There's a World War Three, which, while destructive, humanity manages to survive.

There might be a glancing history with another alien race - those one eyed, tentacle monsters that show up now and then. And perhaps the story of the psychic monsters and the plant beings is a little more nuanced and complex than we've alluded here.

There's time travel, and alternate universes. Not many, but a few. Time Travel is harder in this universe, people go forward, but it's not so easy to go back, and changing history is seldom done.

Going into the future? America, reaches out into space. So does England, and peculiarly Italy and Mexico. There's an entire history of homemade rockets and space ships built by private companies and rich enthusiasts. Obviously impossible in our world, but in this one, there's a lot of crashed flying saucers, leftover wreckage and technological odds and ends from the Matriarchy, the Venerians, the Metaluna and the Enemy, so maybe that has something to do with it.

The people of Earth go out into the Solar System, meet their long lost cousins. The Solar System is revitalized. This becomes the era of TV shows like Space Patrol, Tom Corbett: Space Cadet, Rocky Jones: Space Ranger. Humanity goes out to the stars together. That the ship from Forbidden World is a saucer suggests to me that the two branches of the human race have reconciled and united, to eventually boldly go where no man has gone before.

And that's it.

Afterward

I recommend these movies. I think you should look up some of them, check them out. Give them a look.

One of the fun things about the Retroverse is that it invites a completely new reading of each film, one from the point of view of the 'aliens' operating on a history and an agenda which may be completely different from what these primitive humans have been misled to think. You can watch these films in new ways, and perhaps see them in a larger context as part of some greater design.

I'll be blunt, a lot of them probably haven't aged well. These films weren't state of the art when they were made, and often they were pretty low budget and shoestring by the standards of the time. We're light years away in terms of special effects, dynamic cinematography, pacing... everything about movies has advance. They're often naively sexist, and good luck finding a person of color anywhere. Their idea of diversity is to have an Italian in the crew. They're very much an artifact of their age.

If you watch them, you can probably have a lot of fun mocking them, groaning at clichés or ridiculousness in the stories, implausibilities in the plots, zippers on the monsters, and strings on the spaceships. It's weird, but I think that the cheesier movies hold up better today, their ridiculousness and shortcuts add more of a sense of fun. I don't mind that, I'm snarky myself. But I think mine is affectionate snark.

But overall, there's something about the science fiction movies of this era. There's an ... optimism, a sense that whatever challenges the world poses, we can overcome. There's a faith in these movies, not in religion, but in humanity and in science. These are movies where people come together to meet their crises, sometimes imperfectly, but they come together. Where the state or the enterprise is not indifferent, but has people's backs. Perhaps it's naive, but its uplifting.

I think Star Trek was the last gasp of that idealistic, optimistic sensibility. Star Trek picked up the torch from the Retroverse and built its own universe. Good for them.

The world was changing by the end of the 1960's, Vietnam, Watergate, the oil crisis and stagflation sapped people's confidence. Suddenly the future wasn't bright, or even clear. There was an era of rudderless dystopian science fiction, stuff that matched the trepidation of the 1970's.

Then in the 80's and 90's, we had Giger's Universe, dystopian landscapes of aliens, terminators and road warriors. These were battered and dusty worlds, a bit worn and weathered, ruled, when they were ruled at all, by authoritarian governments and faceless corporations, neither of which could be relied upon. Instead, people were thrown onto their own resources fighting as individuals, or small beleaguered groups. It reflected a more cynical, more brutal era.

But the sci fi of the 50's and 60's, I think there was something special there. I hope you've enjoyed this brief tour of the Retroverse, a cinematic universe in hindsight, built of ancient civilizations, gleaming silver rocketships, flying saucers, brave men and alien women.

The End

When the Romans Sailed to America

The Challenge of the Atlantic Ocean

Here's one of those big historical 'what ifs', popular in alternate histories: What if the Roman Empire had conquered America?

In alternate history, there's a lot of Roman Empire 'what ifs,' mostly along the lines of What if Rome hadn't collapsed, but it includes all sorts – what if they'd beaten back the barbarians, conquered Persia, expanded into Africa, gone north, gone south, what if they'd invented the steam engine, discovered gunpowder etc. etc.

I think it's that historical paradox – the Romans built an Empire that practically encompassed the known world as they saw it, as Europeans saw it, and then it all fell apart. We keep asking ourselves why? And we keep playing with the idea of what else they could have done.

So why couldn't they find America? Establish Nova Roma? All that jazz? What stopped them?

There are those that claim that they did. Or that their predecessors did. There are stories of finding Phoenician ruins, or at least Phoenician coins, claims that some pile of rocks resembles Greek construction, or a petroglyph is a Roman eagle.

Mostly, they're crazy folk. It's proven that the Vikings found their way to North America, and there's a good case that

Polynesians might have made it to the coast of South America.

But all the rest? Zheng La's Chinese Treasure fleet? Japanese? St. Brendan or St. Patrick? The Romans? The Greeks? Phoenicians? Moors? Nope.

Here's the thing.

It's possible.

But it's just not easy. Not even a little.

Here we'll explore both of those things. We'll show why and how it's not easy, and why it wasn't done. And we'll try and carve a pathway, to show how it might have been done, with a little historical tweak, here or there.

The general model for this kind of thing happening is that some Phoenicians, or Greeks, or Romans or whoever, are sailing along outside the pillars of Hercules, and zap a storm comes up and blows them all the way to the Americas.

That's not going to happen.

There's a few reasons – first the Ancients were great sailors… for a given value of 'great.' Basically, they sailed the Mediterranean, which was a pretty placid safe sea to sail around in. Lots of land close by in any direction, predictable stable currents, predictable stable winds, and calm sheltered seas.

The Ancients weren't deep water sailors, mostly, when sailing around the Med, they hugged the coastlines. Maybe after a few centuries or millennia, once they'd gotten to know the place very well, they might take a few shortcuts zipping back and forth. But by and large, they never went more in the Med than a few days out of sight of land. And really, they didn't need to. And honestly? It would have been hard. It's theoretically possible to cross back and forth along the entire

Med without coming in sight of land, but you'd really have to work hard to do it.

It was the same thing with the Red Sea, the Black Sea, the Nile, the Persian Gulf. Now it's true that the Ancients did go beyond the Med. Hanno the Navigator may have circumnavigated Africa. We definitely know that Phoenician and Greek traders during the Bronze Age were travelling as far as England and Denmark. Ancient sailors also travelled as far as India. But the point of all of this is that when venturing into Ocean waters, they were all hugging the coast, sticking in sight of land. Which makes sense – if you're looking for Amber and Tin from Denmark… there's no reason to go into the deep ocean. Your route is going to hug the coastlines.

So I think that's why the usual scenario is to just get blown out in a storm.

Here are the problems:

First, the Ancients had really crap boats. They were fine for tooling around in the Med, no problem, or for coastal jaunts. But they weren't constructed for the Atlantic Ocean.

For one thing, they used combinations of sails and oars, neither of which were great.

If you're travelling, in whole or in part by rowing, then you need a lot of manpower on board, which means you need a lot of food and water on board, or you need to resupply frequently. Long voyages out of sight of land without resupply for your hungry rowers… not a good idea. The Egyptians, Greeks, Romans, Phonecians, etc., all kept large crews of rowers, and no more than a few days supply of food and water. Food and water take up space and have weight. A month or two month's supply to survive a long voyage is a lot of space and weight, and you end up needing a bigger ship to carry it all, which means you need more rowers, and therefore a more food and water, which means an even bigger ship and more rowers. You see the issue. So ships travelled light on supplies and heavy on manpower and weren't at sea too long. That's a big problem with 'being accidentally blown by a storm.' No one who is doing a regular coast hugging jaunt is provisioning their ships for a long spell, so assuming that they get blown out by a storm… they're all dead of dehydration or starvation within a week, months before they can end up anywhere.

While the ancients had sails, let's just be polite and say they weren't great. They were comparatively small, poorly rigged, and couldn't tack into the wind. There was a reason that the ancients relied so much on muscle power.

The big problem though, was in the ancient approach to ship-building in the Mediterranean, which was broadly oriented towards 'mortice and tenon' basically, tongue and hole, like Lego blocks. The ancients would build the skin or the hull of the ship, literally from sewn or joined planks, and then build in an interior skeleton to reinforce it. That was fine for the Mediterranean, and if it started to come apart, well you could try and make it to the nearest land, which usually wasn't too far off.

But the Atlantic was rough dangerous sea in normal times, with constant pounding ocean waves, erratic currents and more erratic winds. Christopher Columbus, with over a thousand year of ship improvements, went out with three ships and lost one along the way. The Atlantic, under normal conditions, would slowly pound a classical Phoenician or Roman ship to pieces in a matter of days. Throw a ship like that into an Atlantic storm, particularly one powerful enough to drive a ship out into the deep ocean towards a new continent… and its game over.

So there's just no way.

Which explains why we are all sitting in England and France right now, given that it's completely impossible?

Well, obviously, it was done, or could be done. You needed to change your technology. In the post-Roman era, people began building ships differently, starting with a keel and ribs, the skeleton first, and then building the rest of it around that skeleton. That produced much stronger ships. The Romans and other ancients weren't doing that, but they could have, if they'd wanted or needed to.

And after Rome, some cultures did manage to brave the Atlantic and get out into the deep sea. But they were motivated.

Take the Norse. Basically, they were a people who were living in a series of sheltered fjords off the Atlantic. The fjords were very nice, but they weren't particularly good farmland, or herding land. You could starve to death living there. To make a go of it, the Norse needed sea protein, they needed to fish, so they would fish in the secluded harbors of their fjords where it was safe, and they'd have to venture out into the Atlantic to catch more fish, and get home. That created a culture of boatbuilding and seamanship which could survive the north Atlantic.

Then the medieval warm spell hits, suddenly there's a population explosion, and all those Norse need new living space, and it turns out they've built up a seafaring navigation technology which allows them to sail out and ravage half of Europe.

And they also go out and use that technology to discover Iceland, Greenland and North America. To be fair though those were all short jaunts, a few hundred miles apiece.

The other significant sailing culture were the Basques. Again, they were a relatively poor people, isolated from their neighbors. They started out as whale hunters. At first, they simply watched from the coasts, whaling close to home in the Bay of Biscay. But as whales moved further and further out to sea, the Basques were forced to follow them, eventually evolving impressive blue water ships and skills. The Basques in turn became the foundation of both the Spanish and Portuguese sailing traditions, which were the foundation of the age of explorations.

So what's the moral of the story? (1) It can be done; (2) You need to build that capacity first though; (3) You need motivation to build that capacity; and (4) You got to start small and work your way up.

There's no pathway that gets some Phoenician, Greek or Roman Captain setting out in a rickety mortise and tenon (Lego block) boat full of oarsman and crossing 4500 miles of angry sea in one jump.

So the first step is to get our hypothetical Ancients, Romans, Carthaginians, Phoenicians, Greeks whatever… for now, let's just call them all Romans… get them to build better boats.

But there's no motivation. The boats they have are perfectly adequate for all the places they need to go – the Med and the nearby Atlantic African and European coasts. They don't really have to go offshore very much. It's not like they need to go deep sea fishing or whaling like the Norse and the Basque.

So we need to change history, to get the Romans out into the ocean. And to get them going out regularly enough, steadily enough that they need to raise their boatbuilding game.

Let me introduce you to 'Macaronesia.' That's a real word by the way; it just doesn't get used much. It's loosely the Atlantic version of 'Polynesia, Melanesia, Micronesia' and refers to a cluster of tropical Islands in the Atlantic Ocean.

Stepping Stones into the Atlantic

THE MACARONESIAN ISLANDS

Now, let's take the Canary Islands. The Canary Islands are nice. Seven major islands, a bunch of small islets, roughly 3000 square miles in area, spread east to west across four hundred miles of ocean; the closest island is sixty miles off the African coast. It's down just between Morocco and the former Spanish Sahara (Sahel?)?

From what we know of antiquity, the Islands were first visited by the Phoenicians, roughly 500 BCE, then by the Greeks and Romans. It was relatively well known, but no one cared. There were reports of ruins, but there was no one living there.

Eventually, a thousand or so years later, the local Guanches would settle the place. But in the ancient era, was uninhabited. Still, the Ancients knew about it, and if they wanted to, they could have gone there regularly; they could have set up shop.

But they didn't need or want to. There was nothing the Canary Islands offered then, that couldn't be obtained easier, faster and with less trouble elsewhere. And honestly, there was nothing much there. So the ancients passed them by.

Four hundred and Fifty miles from the coast, but only two hundred and fifty miles from the Canary Islands were the Madeira archipelago. It's half dozen Islands, including one principal one, totaling three hundred square miles. It was unknown to the ancients, not discovered or inhabited until 1450.

Due north of the Madeiras, about six hundred miles, are the eight islands of the Azores, totaling nine hundred square miles. They're about the longitude of Iberia, and nine hundred and fifty miles from the European coast. Also unknown and uninhabited until modern times.

There's also the Cape Verde Islands, the outlier of the group, located three hundred and fifty miles from the coast of Africa, about a thousand miles south of the Canaries.

All of these islands were empty, and with the exception of the Canaries, all of them were unknown to the Ancients.

Biologically, they were never part of either European or African continents, so all of their life, particularly their flora, ended up arriving blown on the wind, in the guts of birds, or drifting up on the shore. So they form a common, fairly uniform biogeographic region, strongly based on pre-Ice age plant species.

But, they would have potentially been discoverable. If, for instance the hypothetical Romans had decided to settle the Canaries, all of them, and were sailing back and forth between all the Canaries and the Mainland, then they might have had a pretty decent shot at discovering and settling the Madeiras. And if they were sailing regularly around the Canaries and Madeiras, then they've got a good chance at finding the Azores. If they settle the Azores, and they're sailing regularly between the Island groups and the mainland, then they're building up a deep sea sailing capacity for dozens or hundreds of miles between Islands, and up to a thousand miles to the mainland.

The Americas are still 4500 miles away, regardless. But if you've got a regular sailing capacity, boats, navigational skills, the whole thing, capable of thousand mile jaunts through blue water… then it starts to get feasible.

So, our Phoenicians/Greeks/Romans might have been able
to develop the ability to reach the new world. In real life, of
course, they found some of the closest Canary Islands went
'Meh!' and promptly forgot about them.

So, what we need is some reason for our Ancients to be really
interested in those Islands. To want to settle them, to
populate them, and to want the rest of them as they find
them.

Why Even Bother? Motivation…

So what's the motivation? Unlike the Norse, they don't need
deep sea fishing to supplement the sparse food production of
the fjords. Unlike the Basques, they don't need whaling.

There aren't mines or minerals there in any significance,
certainly nothing that they can't get easier or closer. A Prison
Colony? The Ancients liked to keep their prisoners close by,
better for public torture and ritual execution. Summer
cottages? Too far. Imperial hubris? Too short term, the next
Emperor or Dictator pulls the plug on a white elephant
project, and that's it.

The truth is that there wasn't anything there that was
attractive, which is why our history turned out the way it did.

So we need to tweak history just a bit. We need to make those
Islands valuable, so they'll be settled, and new Islands will be
found and settled, and a lively seagoing tradition will emerge.
Whatever it is, it needs to have the following qualities:

It needs to be plausible, something that could, hypothetically
have grown or developed there.

It needs to be portable and transportable, something that can
ship and store well. Strawberries are delicious, but after four
weeks in a ships hold, donkey rides, scorching temperatures

and humidity, with no refrigeration or preservation available, what gets to the Emperors table is… fungus and mulch.

It needs to be incredibly valuable. Both to sustain trade, and to encourage exploration and expansion, and for relatively small quantities to make it economic. So literally worth its weight in gold, or better.

It needs to be common to all the Islands. Otherwise no need for the other islands, and therefore no need for excessive sailing.

It needs to be renewable, because if it's just something that can be hunted, harvested or mined out of existence, that's what they'll do, and then they'll go home and forget about it.

And it has to be easily discoverable, understandable, processable and consumable, because there is no one out on those islands to show you how to weave it, cultivate it, powder it or stuff it up your nose.

There were, through history, a lot of substances like this which drove trade and trade networks. In fact, in this age of bulk commerce where we are shipping millions of tons of dirt cheap stuff like wheat or iron ore across the planet, it may seem strange – but this sort of 'super-valuable' product represents most of the trade in human history.

Take Frankincense and Myrrh, these were incenses – aromatics. Frankincense literally means 'Incense of the Franks' or more accurately 'Incense of Nobles.' What these things were was basically smelly congealed lumps of tree sap. But sweet smelling fragrant lumps of tree sap which retained their sweet odors for a long time. In historical eras when washing was not common and body odours were an issue, these things were a big deal. These lumps of tree sap had medicinal and religious and spiritual properties, because obviously, you wanted your temples to smell nice, you wanted your funerals and ceremonies and ritual offerings to smell nice. These substances originated in Southern Arabia and Somalia, and were so prized that they were literally, weight for weight, more valuable than gold. When it came to the three wise men in Bethlehem, the gold was the trashy cheap gift. They were carried in trading networks as far as India and France. Of course, their use was well established in Southern Arabia before it spread.

Silk is another one, the demand for silk from China was the entire basis of European/Asian trade, it literally bankrupted the Roman Empire, a thousand years later, it helped to drive the age of exploration.

Spices were also huge, tiny quantities form India and Indonesia were incredibly expensive. It was so valuable that during the age of exploration, the Dutch sent four ships from the Netherlands to the Molucca Islands to seek spices. Two of those ships were lost – basically, half the cost of the expedition, right down the drain. But the two ships that made it back were so incredibly profitable that, despite the costs and the losses, everyone involved became incredibly wealthy. That gives you the idea of the crazy economics involved.

Then, during the age of exploration, we saw these incredible booms in Tobacco, in Sugar, in Tea and Coffee, in Chocolate, each of them literally exploding with incredible demand, crazy prices, distorting world economies and populations, turning the world on its ear. The map of the world that we know exists because of the crazed demand for these substances.

The modern equivalent, of course, is drugs – cocaine, opium, heroin, meth, etc. Commodities that all show the same historical features, with demand and prices so high that they overcome the modern obstacles – mainly law enforcement.

So, basically, what we need is a Roman era equivalent of cocaine. Does that blow your mind?

How about actual cocaine? Sorry, no. Cocaine is a refinement of coca leaf extract. Coca plants are well established in South America from Bolivia, through the Andes into Colombia. Too far away, and requires too much processing.

Opium and heroin, same story – that's from poppies from central Asia. Too far away and too much processing.

Tobacco is North America. Tea is India. Sugar is out. There aren't any potential aromatics like Frankincense and Myrrh in West Africa or the islands, besides which, the Middle East already has the aromatics trade sewn up, it would be hard to break into.

What about coffee?

Coffee was practically the cocaine of its day. We're used to it now, we have had four hundred years to get used to it, we drink pots of it every day, we have chains of stores and shops that do nothing but sell coffee, we have aisles of it in grocery stores.

Coffee may have been consumed locally in Ethiopia as far back as 900 AD, but the earliest historical records go back only to about 1400. It emerged in the Ethiopian area, spread steadily but rapidly into the Middle East. Coffee trade reached Italy by about 1600, some of the delay being limited supplies, and of course the constant warfare in the region between the Ottomans, the Arabs and the Europeans. It was a lucrative source of wealth and guarded closely, coffee beans were sterilized before being sold. It wasn't until 1670 that live coffee beans were smuggled out. After that, it was planted or replanted in hospitable tropical areas, notably Colombia and Indonesia.

By the 1700's, Europe was consuming huge quantities of coffee, and was twitchy as hell. Coffee became the social focus around which French salons and salon culture emerged.

This lead to nonstop discussions and discourse, laying the seeds of the French revolution.

As I've said, we've had four hundred years to get used to it – but what if it hit out of the blue. What about a culture or civilization that was having it for the first time? Would it be valuable? Would it be sought out? Would it be mind blowing?

The genus Rubiaceae, also known as the coffee family, originates in the Eocene, probably about 45 or 50 million years ago, and eventually achieved worldwide distribution, mostly in the tropics.

Coffee itself probably originated in Madagascar. There are seven discovered species of Coffee plant there, which seems to be more genetic diversity than the rest of the world put together. We can assume that Coffee plants somehow crossed the Indian Ocean divide, and ended up in the Kenyan and Ethiopian highlands. However, they spread across Africa. Two species were found in the Cameroon highlands. There's a Liberian species which is fairly economically lucrative.

Now, how do Coffee plants manage to jump from Madagascar to Africa, to get from the Kenyan highlands, to Cameroon, to Liberia? I'm assuming the mechanism of transmission in bird guts. Maybe not common, but it happens often enough to jump and establish viable populations.

So if coffee makes at least three major jumps, it's very possible it could make a fourth or fifth.

So our hypothetical flex is this: Coffee Liberica is an established plant growing on or around the lower west coast of Africa, in Liberia and presumably neighboring states. It ends up in the guts of migratory birds who end up dropping it on the Cape Verde Islands, where it takes root and thrives. Migratory bird populations nesting on, and travelling back and forth among the Macaronesia islands transmit it to the

Canaries, the Madeiras and the Azores. Local conditions and lack of herbivores to eat it allow it to take root and thrive.

The coast of Africa around this region is much too dry for coffee plants and there's too much competition and too many herbivores. So what we get are isolated populations of coffee plants all over the Macaronesia islands.

The Cause that Refreshes

Having picked our location, and having picked our 'drug' of choice, we can start nailing down the historical timetable.

The Phoenicians started sailing through the Mediterranean beginning in 1200 BC. The Phoenician colony of Cadiz was established in Spain around 1100 BC. Oddly, Carthage, closer to home, was only founded in 900 BC. By about 700 BC, it had become the dominant Phoenician state in the west. There's some indication that Phoenician traders and explorers may have been sailing out beyond, along the coasts of Africa and Europe.

Approximately 500 BC, the Carthaginians send a fleet of 60 ships under Hanno the Navigator to explore the coast of Africa. The Carthaginians were a mercantile people, so the expedition likely had trade opportunities in mind.

Hanno is our first record of the Canary Islands, although Hanno reports that he finds the ruins of great buildings. The Island is uninhabited. It's possible that these are the ruins of previous Phoenician stations. It's unlikely that these ruins would have lasted a long time, so let's say that the Canaries were found at least twice, maybe a few times, between 800 BC and 500.

Ever been to sea? Old school sea, on biremes, or old style sailing ships? Not cruise liners, but the sort of boats where it was brutal manual labor and cramped conditions every day? I'll tell you a secret. The food sucks Basically, there's nothing fresh, no fresh meat, no fresh plants, it's all dried, harsh stuff that's meant to last, it's on the ocean so there's a lot of humidity to make things go bad, storage is hard, even wine and water starts tasting pretty foul after a day, insects get into everything.

When you read the old sailing accounts, the recurring thing was the minute sailors had the chance to put into any kind of land, they were running about frantically looking for anything that might be edible – funny looking plants, berries, nuts, bird eggs, lizards, tortoises. Sailors were not fussy, anything they could cook that wasn't shipboard rations. Shipboard food was awful, so they'd try anything.

There's stories about Darwin and the voyage of the Beagle, and when the Beagle sailors got to the Galapagos, they were gorging on tortoises. They brought live tortoises with them to eat later. Have you ever seen those things? Who in their right mind would look at that and think, 'Yum.' But that was the sailor's life – hunger and hideously awful, dried, soggy, moldy, insect infested, rotting food, stuff chosen not for its taste or edibility, but solely for its ability not to go bad.

Which means, of course, that when Hanno's sailor's, or his predecessors, put in at the Canaries, they're just going wild looking for fresh meat and vegetables and fresh water. And there's stuff to eat. There's giant lizards, giant rats, giant tortoises (for a given value of giant – we're talking critters the size of chickens and turkeys), which are easy to catch. There's fresh water.

It's the right season, they're collecting berries, seeds, leafs, roots, anything that looks like it might make a meal. And there's these trees which are producing a funny kind of nut or bean that looks like it could be edible. Maybe if you boiled it or something. These guys are crazy hungry for anything that's not ships rations.

So they boil em up, and they have them with fried lizard, and the next thing you know, they're climbing the trees, they're talking nonstop, they're swabbing the decks, re-rigging the whole fleet, maybe sewing up some new sails, hey does the flagship need paint job, let's do that! It's a kick.

So Hanno and his men gather them up, and they take as much as they can with them. Because it's a long voyage across strange shores, and they're nowhere sure of welcomes or places to provision. So an uninhabited island with magic beans, they're going to remember that place.

Hanno goes out, he comes back. He stops off and gathers more. He goes back to Carthage. Carthage, in our history, and in this history, establishes a trade route around the coast of Africa, with the equatorial kingdoms.

In our history, that trade route peters out eventually. Maybe it was just cheaper to trade overland across the desert. More likely, it ends when the Romans burn down Carthage, the sideline dies on the vine.

But this history is a little different.

The word gets around about the magic beans. Subsequent sailors travelling back and forth make a point of picking up coffee beans, maybe even making a special trip. Carthage sets up a way station there to provision its trading expeditions with the southern kingdoms. Coffee is very accessible with a semi-permanent establishment. The trading station harvests coffee from the other Islands. They're able to harvest in season. There's a regular yield.

Coffee becomes a small scale but extremely valuable luxury trade commodity. Enough to justify making regular trips.

The Fall of Atlantis – Page 94

Now, here's the thing with coffee liberica. It's 'infrastructure' type coffee. We're not talking bushes here. Liberica produces 20 meter trees. That's about sixty, seventy feet. You'll get a real good crop of beans from one of those trees. But if you want my thinking ... it takes a long time to grow a seventy foot tree, particularly at the outer peripheries of the plant's range. Way too slow to cultivate like you would a normal crop.

So basically, the Canary harvests start simple exploitation. Go out, hunt around, find a tree or grove and harvest. But we're not talking cultivation or management. Initially, you might see short-sighted asshats cutting down the trees to collect the beans. But the smarter in the bunch realize if they don't cut the trees down, they can show up at the right time every year to collect. And of course, the way to increase harvest is to just keep finding new trees.

So the Island group gets pretty explored. Maybe even some settlement. Definitely some settlement. You need people on site to harvest, of course. After it gets known about, eventually, poachers and smugglers are going to come looking. So you want to keep a presence year round. After all, these are pretty valuable beans; want to keep an eye on them. There's the seeds (excuse the pun) of a blue water sailing capacity emerging there.

Now, fast forward just a little bit. There's a thriving coffee economy, maybe even coffee arboculture based around the Canaries. It's valuable as hell. Demand always outruns supply. The demand is huge.

Maybe someone decides to go sailing around, looking for more islands. After all, there's eight of them in the Canaries, finding a ninth would be like finding a pot of gold.

Sail around, look for clues. Even if you didn't sight it, you might spot birds flying in or out of odd directions, perhaps leaves or branches in the water, where they shouldn't be. Even bad clues or sheer mysticism might keep people looking.

Then, somewhere say between 400 BCE and 300 CE, Madeira is discovered. Now, Madeira isn't quite so promising. Maybe a few hundred square miles in all. Two principle islands.

But low and behold, there's a population of Coffee Liberica trees there, just waiting to be harvested. Probably not a great population. But there's a huge demand for coffee, worth its weight in gold and all that. So the discovery of a second set of coffee islands, which might represent a significant increase in production from 10 to 30% (depending), is a big, big thing. Also, an even bigger thing - it's an unclaimed set of coffee islands. A wonderful resource. So lots and lots of interest.

Now, it starts to get cool. You have seafarers dancing 60 miles out into deep water, bouncing hundreds of miles around the islands of the Canaries. Then you've got them 280 miles out, booting around Madeira. Maybe communicating regularly back and forth with the Canaries. Or shipping directly over to Europe - open water journeys of 250 to 500 miles. Impressive.

That's where you're starting to develop blue water skills. A 500 mile trip is no great shakes; America is still thousands of miles away. But when you're making 200 or 300 or 500 mile blue water trips, you start to get to know the currents, the winds, the seasons, etc. Your territory is local, but you're getting a picture window of the local that you can generalize from ... After all, those currents and winds are going somewhere.

But the really mind blowing thing here is an intellectual leap. "There are other islands" The Canaries might have just been their little one off. One is a special number.

But two is an unreal number. The thing with two - once you get to two, then you get to the possibility of three or four, or all kinds of other numbers. Once you get past the notion that something is not unique, singular, a category of 'one' - and are coming to grips with the idea that there could be more than the one ... like two ... that opens the door.

And in this case, that door opens onto a gold mine. Because coffee is incredibly valuable, and incredibly hard to get a hold of. If coffee is not just confined to the Canaries, but grows in another place ... it might grow in other places, too.

There's now an incentive to start looking. To sail down around the coast of Africa, seeing if there's more coffee plants there. There might be. They'd have to get pretty damned far to get to Liberia. But they get there.

But before Liberia, there's a good chance of getting to the Cape Verde Islands. These are 350 miles off the coast of Africa. About 10 islands. Fifteen hundred square miles. Would the coast huggers find the Cape Verde Islands? Well, these are guys who have a proto-deep sea tradition, and are used to making 250 and 500 mile voyages, and they're a long way out. And they're looking for islands or signs of islands, because, after all, the coffee trees only grow on islands so far.

Anyway, between the Canaries, Madeira, Cape Verde and possibly some harvest on the African coast, there's a pretty thriving and lucrative coffee trade going on. You with me so far?

Here's the big thing. Exploration, and luck, have paid off. There's a set of brass rings that have been collected. Sure, there's lots of failures; unlucky sods who found nothing, lost their shirts, or died swallowing their tongues at sea. But you know how it is - the same urge that keeps people gambling would keep people on the lookout.

Now, the Azores. About a thousand square miles, the islands are scattered over about 350 miles width. It's about 850 miles west of Portugal. 950 south west of Morocco. This would be our biggest jump - but we are now looking at coastal voyages of maybe 1500 or 2000 miles, and several areas of deep sea crossings between 250 and 550 miles. So it's a jump, but not an unmanageable one.

Within this time frame, between say 300 BCE and 100 CE, you have a thriving set of island economies going, devoted to a very lucrative commodity, with an evolved tradition not only of sea craft but sea knowledge, and a culture which is open to the idea that there could be more islands or more of value out there.

You've got this incredibly lucrative string of Carthaginian colonies established on these island groups, producing coffee and facilitating the Africa trade, sailing back and forth, carrying on longer and more ambitious voyages among each other, even thousand mile trips back to the mainland. One that is developing a reasonable knowledge of coastal geography, and offshore winds, currents and seasons.

Now that is the sort of sea tradition in which a lost, blundering, or storm-driven ship could end up surviving all the way to a landing in the new world. And that's the sort of sea tradition where they'd have a rat's ass chance of finding their way home. And that's the sort of sea tradition where the local cultures might see enough potential and opportunity to try and make something of it.

The world is a little bit more interesting. Coffee is introduced to the Mediterranean. There's small quantities but it's sold to the Greeks, the Romans, its special prized drink. The Mediterranean world is changed a little bit, maybe not too much. Carthage is wealthier.

Africa has probably changed a little, with the more regular trade, the more increased volume. But we don't know enough to say.

The continuing discovery of a handful of Macaronesian archipelagos, the Azores, and its 30 islands, and the potential wealth that comes from a virgin new coffee Island probably inspires a lot of fortune seekers.

Searching for Brave New Fortunes

There's soothsayers giving the locations of new Islands and new fortunes, smugglers and pirates claiming that their coffee comes from previously unknown and still mysterious islands, learned men of letters proving to each other that there must be more islands out there. There's dreams, dreamers and half ass lunkheads. There's the desperate, gambling on that incredibly long shot. The ambitious seeking to make their fortune, etc.

So, during the period of exploration, they keep setting out to sea... and it worked to some extent, after all, they did find the Azores and Cape Verde.

Mostly, they just die at sea. They die a lot. Their ships founder in bad weather, they spring a leak and sink, the crew mutinies, they get lost. Basically, they die in profusion, in numbers. Many of the ships that go out don't come back. Of those that do, many come back empty handed. It's a lot of dying at sea or coming back busted.

Now, there's an interesting thing – the winds and currents in the Atlantic aren't random, they fall into predictable steady patterns, based on locations and seasons. Around the Macaronesian Islands, there's a circular current called the

Volta Del Mar which cycles around. Circular currents are called gyres.

Now, the interesting thing about the Volta del Mar, is that if you ride it, it can take you right into a westerly current, that will take you directly to the upper coast of Brazil. All you have to do is stay alive and ride the current, and you'll get there.

The Volta del Mar and that westerly current, by the way, is the reason that Portugal, instead of Spain, ended up with Brazil. One of those quirks of history.

A lot of how different European countries ended up dominating which stretches of coastline actually has to do with which currents they were riding, and where these currents would ship them up.

Now under those circumstances, I expect two things to happen.

The seamen who survive to come back empty handed will come back rich in knowledge. Mostly that knowledge will be that spending three weeks bopping around the empty ocean really sucks. But there'll be a modicum of accumulated awareness of winds and currents. So it's likely that they'll figure out the currents, particularly the Volta del Mar, and perhaps develop that as an institutional knowledge - i.e., the traditions and insights that everyone defaults too.

At that point, late, very late in the age of exploration and consolidation, you might have, the occasional really gifted and unlucky fool who ends up in Brazil, in one of those 'Incredible Voyages' which we usually associate with team ups of wily cats and broken down dogs travelling thousands of miles to find their absent minded owners.

The currents are right, the winds are right, and presumably they've brought a modicum of skill and preparation. And mostly, if they survive the trip out there, they die out there. It's really really hard to get back.

The problem is that the winds and the currents around there only run in one direction. You can't just get in your boat and sail back the way you came. To find currents and winds heading back east, you have to head either far to the north, or far to the south. That's thousands more miles of sailing, along the coasts, along strange, alien coasts full of strange hostile peoples. That's kind of uphill.

I suppose that there's some possibility of a Phoenician settler colony composed of stranded sailors, that merges with the locals. It might last fifty or a hundred years, unless it's very lucky. But I'm not going to worry about that for now.

By the time the first Punic war rolls around, about 264 BC, the Canaries are an economic/political metropolis, with the rest of Macaronesia and an indefinite portion of the African coast as hinterland, and Coffee is the Carthaginian refreshment.

Probably the Punic Wars roll out mostly the way they did in our history. I don't think there's enough money in the Coffee/Africa trade to really change the outcomes.

Rome eventually destroys Carthage, and in our history, that's definitely the end of the Africa sea trade.

But the Macaronesia Coffee Trade is incredibly lucrative. So maybe the Canary Island colony gathers up all its fellow Islanders and fleets and establish their own independent Phoenician nation.

Or maybe the Romans just roll in, say "Under new management, just keep doing whatever you were doing," and the locals say 'Yes, Sir!"

Probably doesn't make a lot of difference, because the whole point of these Islands is to feed the insatiable demand for Coffee in the Mediterranean. So they're either going to be part of the Roman empire, or a tributary kingdom, but they're in bed with Rome, one way or the other.

Okay, so we've got an active, capable seagoing culture which is building boats that can survive the Atlantic seas. We've got a lucrative market. We've got even got the occasional boob or shipload of fools showing up alive in Brazil.

Is that as far as we can go?

Not quite. Because there is a chance to get back, maybe. The Macaronesian Carthaginians get to be very good sailors. Incredibly good Atlantic sailors with incredibly good ships. They'd probably be in demand up and down the Atlantic coasts, they'd be paying attention to the winds and currents.

If you were sailing regularly around the coasts of Gaul and Britain what you might notice is that the winds in the summer blow east, they'd be coming in from the west.

So assuming that you're some lucky Phoenician, incredibly lucky, and your ship, or hell your fleet made it all the way to Brazil in relatively good shape. And assuming you wanted to get home, and you had some knowledge of these easterly winds up north.. Maybe you could take a chance.

Maybe you'd sail up the coast of Brazil, and then up the West Indies, up Central America, until you got to somewhere between Puerto Rico and Florida, and decided, with a fully provisioned and reinforced ship, to try it.

It would be probably two or three years. It would be an incredible feat of seamanship, of perseverance. A legendary effort of skill, daring and amazing luck.

But it could be done.

Now, I imagine anyone who makes a journey like this is going to talk it up the wazoo, so the stories will be amazing and epic and all that, extravagant as hell.

And…. So what?

An incredible voyage is pretty awesome. But hey, we went to the moon back in the 60's and 70's. We did it a bunch of times. Do you see a moon colony?

That's because all we got back from the Moon was rocks, and we have plenty of rocks on Earth.

So if there's an incredible voyage, that's very nice. But it doesn't necessarily mean that the Romans are going to see a future in it. It may be a one off trip.

Taking the Long Way Home

Let's back up a few paces. Our unnamed Phoenician hero. He or She ended up in Brazil along the coast. He's sailing along the coast. They meet people. They'll encounter the Terra culture along the Brazilian coast. They may encounter Central American cultures, the Taino, the Arawak, maybe even the early Maya.

They're a Phoenician from an intense trading culture, their whole life will have been about the super-lucrative coffee trade. So they'll maybe keep an eye out for coffee. Maybe this new world is the motherlode of coffee, and they'll come back with a kingdom's worth of beans in their holds and retire as wealthy men.

That won't happen. There's no coffee in the new world. But they'll keep an eye out.

And there are interesting things that they might bring home.

There's peanuts. And tomatoes. There's potatoes, sweet potatoes, cassava, maize, beans, squash, sunflower seeds. There's hutia as a small food animal. Don't laugh, if potatoes made it back to Rome and cultivation, it would be a game changer.

I'll be honest. The Phoenicians won't care even a bit. There's not enough money in potatoes. Cultivating them would be a social and economic game changer. But they won't think that way. They're thinking about cash, something that can turn a quick book, produce some big money.

Anything like that out there?

Gold, but they got gold back home.

There are a few things. Coca, the plant that produces cocaine. You actually need substantial processing to get to Cocaine. But Coca leaves themselves will produce a mild high.

There's Cacao, which is the bean that produces chocolate, and which the Mayans use for a narcotic drink, very popular with the ruling classes.

There's Tobacco, another one of those 'world changers' that's been around so long we hardly pay attention to it, but it might potentially be quite big.

There's chili peppers, there's vanilla. There's a few other possibilities.

So… our hero makes it home with a hold full of potatoes, cassava and whatnot to keep them alive, and as much chocolate, coca, tobacco and whatever else they can stuff in their holds, to hopefully turn some kind of profit on what is otherwise a disastrous three year voyage through hell.

Now, if we were all Vulcans, probably that would be the end of things. Considering the immense, distances, the time, the costs, it's hard to imagine coming back with a valuable enough cargo to justify the trip, much less justify any other or continuing trade.

But there's this thing called irrational exuberance. Coffee was explosively lucrative. The Macaronesians have spent generations always looking for and dreaming of the next big thing, the new coffee islands to be discovered, the next 'coffee' crop. There'll be a lot of interest in the new world and its commercial potential. There might be quite a lot of effort into learning to sail efficiently back and forth from the new world, figuring out the currents and winds, figuring out how to survive the trip, finding or developing the next 'coffee.'

Some enterprising Phoenician might even decide to try it the other way – gold is gold after all, what cool and valuable old world wares, or cheap tat, they can pawn off on the natives for their gold or jewels, in order to get fabulously wealthy.

One thing that strikes me that might be at work, particularly during and lingering after the discovery phase, is 'gamblers fever.' I'm sure that there's another term for it - intermittent reinforcement. The fact that a chance pays off once in a while, or might pay off persuades people to keep playing. This is why people buy lottery tickets or throw their life savings away at a casino (well, there's also the doubling down phenomena - basically, when someone's made the mistake of throwing a lot of money down the well there's a strong impulse to keep throwing down money, otherwise you have to admit that all your time and money and effort up to that time has been for nothing).

But ultimately, I think it's just too expensive a proposition. The scale of investment is too huge, too risky, for local entrepreneurs, even canny Phoenicians.

No matter how much hypothetical wealth is out there, the difficulties of getting it back, and the exponential costs of setting up a trade network would be outside the economic capacity of the Canary metropolis or its entrepreneurs. There's just not enough wealth to make that kind of investment and no real motivation to do so. In particular, the Canary metropolis might want to have a whole new supply of coffee/specialty trade good... but on the other hand, it doesn't want competitors, or the price to collapse.

So eventually, it just dies on the vine.

Honestly, what we have here are a chain of events of branching pathways, and there are many opportunities for things to die on the vine every step of the way.

So there's a new world boom, and then there's a new world bust as all the adventurers and investors lose their shirts. The New World becomes a part of the Roman records, Cicero or whoever writes about it. But no one pays attention to it. It's just this historical curiosity, until a dozen centuries later, when Chris Columbus, or his equivalent sets sail with a lot better idea of what he's going to find.

Over in the new world, there's a few archeological sites with Phoenician or Roman artifacts and relics, maybe a few loan words in local languages, maybe some DNA, maybe a few little cultural odds and ends.

That's not bad.

But we can take it further.

Imperial Rome Spreads Wings

This is going to upset the Libertarians in the audience, but here's the thing: The conquest and colonization of the new world was not by bands of plucky entrepreneurs setting up sugar or tobacco plantations. It was by states and empires. They were the only ones that had the resources to underwrite these projects, to make massive investments, including long term investments. Columbus was underwritten by the Spanish Royals, and whether they did it personally or with the state treasury is irrelevant. That was the only way it could happen. There was direct State activity, there were agents and agencies, freebooters, license holders, every kind of arrangement, but it had to be the state somewhere.

There is a state here.

The Roman Empire. The only state that might have the resources to set up such a trade network - including posts and resupply stations, would be Rome. And there's no military or political reason to do so. It's certainly not a paying proposition, at least not in the short run. So what it comes down to is boondoggle, the senseless whim of some crazed emperor, pouring the wealth of the state into such a venture. You'd need a lot of money, a lot of wealth and input, for very little to show for it. So the only reason it would happen would be misinformation, skewed assessments, really bad decision making and an immense fortune disposed of recklessly.

Then again, it's an Emperor, maybe he's willing to spend lifetime's worth of money to impress his friends with Chocolate Malt, or low grade pseudo-cocaine. Maybe he's got some really insanely long term vision. Or he just wants to.

So you could, hypothetically see a Roman presence and a series of Roman outposts, way stations, trading stations and resupply depots from the coast of Brazil to the Caribbean and beyond, established and maintained at possibly ruinous expense.

That will probably last until the change of Emperors.

Or maybe it makes enough of a profit, produces enough return to keep on going for a while.

And it's unlikely to have much of a meaningful effect. After all, Rome and China knew of each other, and there was some limited exchange through the silk road. There was some contact between Meso-American and Andean cultures. But in each case, the contact was mostly insignificant. This could be the same... only more so.

It's almost certain that the Roman Empire will decline. They only occupied Britain for forty years. They were in Mesopotamia for a generation or so. The Empire declines, it retreats from its furthest flung holdings. The New World adventure is abandoned.

But even so, you could have some very interesting things happening.

The potential effects on Rome could be huge.

Forget about the Chocolate Malts. The longer there's sustained contact, the more sustained contact, the more likelihood that new world crops and food sources will make it over. These aren't things that Roman Emperors or Legionaries care about. These aren't things that Phoenician mercenaries care about. They're the small unimportant things that change the world.

Potatoes, Sweet Potatoes, Maize, Cassava, Squash, these things can grow where Roman crops won't grow, they can feed more people per acre than Roman crops. This means new farms, new agricultural land coming into play. It means more food, more people, better fed people. More farmers and landholders, more wealth, more economic activity, a more robust. The result could be a wealthier, more dynamic Roman Empire. Perhaps one that doesn't withdraw from England, but expands to Ireland. That expands into Germany to Denmark, that presses into the Crimea and Ukraine, and down the Mediterranean into Arabia. Perhaps this triggers waves of innovation, new ideas and methods to address the Empire's problems and limitations.

These crops, when they came to Europe and Africa during the age of discovery were revolutionary. They changed the world for us, in our own history, in the last five hundred years. They would certainly transform the world of two thousand years ago.

Rome will probably still fall, in the end, it was simply too big for the logistics and communication systems of its time. But it may get an extra century or two. It may rack up new conquests and victories.

What comes after Rome, the feudal states, the new Kingdoms and Empires, with different and more robust agricultural foundations, may have entirely different trajectories. Islam, for instance, might have a lot harder time conquering beyond Arabia.

On the other side of the Ocean, the impacts on the New World could be extraordinary and open ended.

The time frame we are looking at for possible New World contact, between say 200 BC to 200 AD puts you into the late Pre-Classical, early Classical Era. You'd miss just miss the Olmecs, it's a bit too late for them. But you'd encounter Meso-American cultures from Panama to Mexico, including the Maya in their classical period. You'd encounter the Terra Preta Civilization in Brazil.

The Roman Empire wouldn't necessarily be offering new crops. But it has a number of attributes that could be game changers. Chicken, for instance. Sheep or Goats. Horse and Cattle. Draft labor animals like horse or cattle could be massive game changers, allowing the Meso-Americans or the Terra Preta access to far more 'horsepower' than humans could produce, as well as new sources of protein.

Metallurgy could be huge, catapulting Meso-America from Neolithic or early limited Bronze technology to full-fledged Iron Age societies. Literacy and written language could be introduced, and proliferate.

It's hit and miss what might pass across the Atlantic. Chickens might be easy to transport. Horses and cattle might be expensive, difficult and a pain in the ass. Even if they do cross the Atlantic, the Romans might not let go of these animals – horses may be too big an advantage in cavalry to allow the locals a breeding population. I'm sure that the Romans would be happy to sell Iron and steel, but perhaps they might not share the secrets of smelting and metallurgy.

Meso-American civilizations came and went. The Maya rose and fell. Empires came and went. But these civilizations built on each other's accomplishments. Any boost from Roman contact or trade could create profound changes, both in Meso-America and well beyond.

And what about the Roman outposts in the new world.

Where would they be?

The travel route that gets established starts from Macaronesia and the Volta del Mar, to the western currents that reach the upper shores of Brazil. From there, The romans sail north along the coast to the Western Antilles, the Caribbean Islands, touching on Meso-America.

They don't want to be vulnerable, so while it's tempting to be close to the Meso-Americans and other trading partners, they also want someplace safe, beyond the reach of the local states. They want to trade with the Maya, they don't want to be owned or bullied by them.

The Roman/Phoenicians in the new world are adept and skillful sailors with advanced ships. That's their big advantage. So they'll build their outposts and fortifications on the

Caribbean islands. It's protected, the locals are no match for them, easily conquered or driven off, they can reach everywhere they want to in the New World. They could conquer or proclaim dominion over the entire West indies, from Trinidad to the Bahamas, including Cuba, Hispaniola, Jamaica, Puerto Rico. They could build installations, ports, towns, cities.

Rome occupied England for three hundred and fifty years. Eventually, the Legions went home, the locals were on their own, and England got invaded a lot – by the Picts, the Celts, Angles, the Saxons, the Franks, the Normans. That was just sort of how it went, a lot of barbarians moving back and forth, a lot of fighting. Everyone had the same technology, more or less. It was just the neighborhood.

But think about this outpost of the Roman Empire over in the new world, based on Cuba or Hispaniola, dominating the whole Island. When Rome withdraws, maybe it's too far to recall most of the legions, most of the farmers and tenants, the civil service the administrators. Maybe just the high ranking officials leave… And things go on without them.

That could be interesting, because while Rome and its provinces and tributaries are all being invaded by barbarians, while Rome is struggling and the Byzantine Empire comes into being, with its own struggles with Barbarians and Rival Empires…

Those Roman outposts in the Caribbean could well just keep on trucking. Think about it. There are no outside barbarians invading. The Romans can easily dominate and overwhelm the locals. The Arawakian people are not united, they're not organized politically, they lack metal weapons or armor, they lack Roman military training or tactics, technology, horses, ships. The Romans can conquer all of them, convert them, enslave them, subjugate them. They could build a new Roman Empire in the new world.

Conquering the Maya, or whoever the predecessors of the Aztec that's a non-starter. These are warlike societies on home ground, and they have numbers. They're also customers. The Romans would be looking at incredible expense and probably bad results.

But steadily taking over the Caribbean, recreating a Roman Empire, or perhaps a version of Carthage, that's doable. Most of the population would still be local Arawakians of course. Over time, the Romans or Phoenicians would simply be a smear of DNA.

But this Roman Empire would be Christian, or a version of Christian. Latin would be the dominant language, or at least the imperial language of religion, government and war. Roman technology, mythology, values and culture would be imprinted upon indigenous cultures. It would evolve over time.

But in 1492, when Columbus or his equivalent shows up, well, he wouldn't be encountering trusting hapless defenseless Indians. He'd and his ships would be taken into custody by the Roman Empire, a sea power with colonies and outposts from Florida and New Orleans to the Amazon, consumed by rivalry with the Aztec and Mayan Empires, with diplomatic relations with the Indians. He'd be dragged before the true Emperor and heir to all the provinces, here and there. He'd have a lot of questions to answer, and his version of Christianity might not pass muster. Now that would be interesting.

The End

A Different Greenland

Where the Ice Never Came

Introduction

Greenland is melting. The largest island on earth, covered by two miles of ice, and it's melting. There's a lot of ice, it's not all going away anytime soon. It will take a long time to melt. But now we're looking at the chance that perhaps, in a few thousand years, we'll see a new Greenland with the ice gone away, a real green land finally coming into being.

We're not going there. Instead, for this thought experiment we will explore: What if Greenland was never covered by Ice? What if it was, for practical purposes, mostly ice free for most of its history? What if it was ice free now?

What would it be like? What animals would roam there? Would there have been people there? Who would they have been, and what would they become? Could there have been a civilization?

Let's explore an alternate Greenland, a Greenland that, for whatever reason, never succumbed completely to the ice.

Vital Statistics

Let's talk Greenland: 2,166,000 square kilometers, or 836,000 square miles, 1570 miles in length north to south, 680 miles at its widest. Stretching from latitude 59, just short of the arctic circle, to latitude 84 a barely 450 miles from the geographic north pole. Greenland is larger than Mexico, Saudi Arabia, the Sudan or Indonesia. It's roughly as large as most of the countries of Western Europe put together.

It's one of the most barren places on Earth, with 95% of it covered by a gigantic ice sheet up to two miles thick. That Ice Sheet, or parts of it, goes back 18 million years, although most of it probably dates back less than ten million years. If all that ice melted tomorrow, the ocean level all over the planet would rise twenty feet.

The Land Beneath the Ice

Do we even know what that Greenland looks like?

As a matter of fact, yes, we do. Greenland's coastal mountain ranges have long been identified by flyovers and satellites. Over the last few decades, starting in the 1970's, deep radar and sonar imaging has slowly but steadily built us a picture of the landscape beneath the ice.

Discoveries are still being made. For instance, in 2013, we identified Greenland's Grand Canyon, 466 miles long, six miles wide, 2600 feet deep. In 2014, a meteor impact crater, larger than Washington and the District of Colombia, was detected in the north of Greenland. We've discovered entire river systems. Ancient fertile soil has been found beneath the ice, hinting at a history of green fields, forests and marshes. It's not a perfect picture, there's still much to fill in. And it might not be perfectly accurate - this is the landscape being pressed down by two miles of ice. If all that ice was gone, there would be some degree of isostatic rebound. But it gives us something to work with.

At this point, we have a decent picture of what Greenland looks like under all that ice. That's the topographic map image on the front cover. This probably gives us a pretty good read on what's likely to be going on with Greenland. There are two major sets of geological features that shape Greenland's geography, and in turn, affect climate, biology and ecology. The mountains and the Central Sea.

Climate and Geography

So, even if we take away the ice, wouldn't we just still have a frozen wasteland? Greenland is pretty far north after all. It practically stretches to the North Pole.

As we've said, Greenland is immense. We think of it as arctic, and not without justification. At its northernmost, latitude 74, it really is one of the closest land masses to the north pole. Only a few small Russian Islands come closer, and then only by a few miles.

But Greenland is 1570 miles from north to south and stretches through to latitude 59. Latitude 59 or 60 is no fun. 60 latitude is officially the dividing line for the Canadian arctic, and it's the dividing line between the populated Alaska panhandle and the frozen Alaska wilderness. North of 60 the image is a lot of tundra and muskeg.

But take a look at a map - Greenland actually stretches well to the south of Iceland, which lies between latitudes 63 and 68. It's comparable to Finland which occupies latitudes 60 to 70. The southernmost point of Greenland is as far south as the northern tip of Scotland, or the mid and southern regions of Sweden and Norway. Latitude 59 includes large forest and lake-filled areas of European Russia and Siberia.

So no, we don't necessarily get a vast empty landscape of barren rock and tundra. It's possible. But that wouldn't be much fun. So let's assume Greenland is going to be much more interesting than that.

Harsh Landscape, the Arctic Desert

In the north, top of the island, let's say roughly 78 to 84 latitude, we've basically got arctic desert - kind of like the Canadian Archipelago. Cold, dry and arid, with very little precipitation. You are six to twelve degrees latitude from the actual north pole. It's facing the open Arctic Ocean, and you've got the polar vortex to keep it chill. It's pretty barren and very close to the popular concept of the high arctic.

You'll get tundra and muskeg, lots of permafrost, no trees, no grasses. There'll be rivers and lakes, but they'll be frozen much of the year. The rivers will run for only a few of months of the year. In the far north, on the topographic maps, there maybe a couple of channels or sea accesses between the Arctic Ocean and that Central Sea where water might flow back and forth, but that's likely to be seasonal.

In short, not very hospitable, and not terribly different from what we have now. Let's assume that this represents about a fifth of Greenland. Old Greenland isn't much different from New Greenland in its far north.

The Eastern Mountains and Plains

The harsh barren landscape change as you move south. Let's look at the mountains, specifically, that range of peaks and highlands running along the Eastern coast, between latitude 67 and 76. Got it? Take a look at the topography map. I'll wait. Done? Okay. Now, these highlands comprise the Watkins Mountain Range, the Crown Prince Frederick Range, the Princess Elizabeth Alps and a few others. They're fairly hefty mountains. Well, somewhat. They're far from the stature of the Himalayas or the Rockies. But they're not bad. The tallest peaks run over 12,000 feet, there are lots over 10,000, and lots more over 5,000.

So, what about these mountains? Well, a few things. First up, they're a climate barrier. Now this gets a little hinky. Normally, seas and oceans are heat sinks. They tend to retain heat and manifest very stable temperatures. So, landscapes next to seas tend to experience moderated (not necessarily moderate) climates. Their temperature slides along a narrow range, they don't get super-hot because of the cool ocean next door, they don't get super cold because of warmer ocean next door. Now, what does this mean for Greenland? Well, probably a mostly good thing, because Greenland isn't warmed by the Gulf stream the way that Iceland and Norway are.

Instead, Greenland gets arctic currents from the cold and nasty side of the Atlantic Ocean, so without the mountain barrier, its inland temperatures would likely be flatter and colder and generally more unpleasant. With the mountains blocking the ocean, you'll get warmer summers and colder winters inland, more temperature extremes.

But hey, if you want moderating bodies of water, there's the Central Sea. Stick a pin in that, we'll come back to it later.

The second thing about Mountains that's really cool, is that - if they're tall enough - they get a snowcap. Glaciers form from condensation and accumulated precipitation at the top of mountains. Sometimes, they'll descend and crawl around like some geologic version of a B-Horror movie, but we won't go there. Now, how tall does a mountain have to be to get itself a snowcap? Depends on a bunch of stuff, the big factors being location and height. Basically, the taller a mountain is, the more chance of a snowcap. Latitude is a factor. Obviously, a tall enough mountain can get a snowcap even at the tropics. Kilimanjaro, for instance, is about 16,000 feet in Africa, and had a snowcap. Same with the Andean mountains near the equator. But further north, it gets easier, you get mountains showing snowcaps at shorter and shorter heights. So, that Greenland range, with its whole passel of mountains between 6,000 and 12,000 feet in height ... probably lots of snowcaps and mountain glaciers. Possibly too many, it's probably why Greenland iced up in our world.

Anyway, so here we are with a lot of mountain glaciers all up and down across about half the length of Greenland's eastern coasts. You know what Glaciers do? Apart from acting like B-movie horror monsters except at geologic speeds. They melt. Not completely, and sometimes not at all. But generally, they spend the winter storing up snow and precipitation, building up their snowcap and crawling down the sides of the mountain. Then spring, summer, fall comes along. You get warmer temperatures and they slowly start to melt. What this gives you is slow steady, glacier fed rivers. Some seasonal flooding, yes. But mostly, it's a steady season long water supply. It doesn't melt all at once, so no flash floods. Rather, it's gradual, so you have a constant stable river system. This is a good thing.

So where does all this fresh glacial water go? Well, most of it, let's say about two thirds, is just going into the Atlantic Ocean. So ... pooh. Hardly seems to be worth the effort, eh? The remaining third goes inwards, to fill a Central Sea. But let's come back to that ...

But if you look on the other side of those Eastern mountains, what we see is that there's a pretty gentle, gradual slope running a eventually to the central sea. So, what does that mean? It means that the water is moving more slowly. With slower movement, the erosional processes aren't as fierce, you've got more silt and sediment deposit along the way, coming all the way down from the mountains, so you get more winding rivers, more lakes, more marshes, more peat bogs, swamps, muskegs, and generally more water in the landscapes. And with the silt and sediment deposit, sands and gravels, you get the makings of more productive, enriched soils.

The east side interior, between the mountains and the Central Sea is likely wet tundra - permafrost in the north, dotted with rivers and lakes, as you move further and further south, that will give way to shrub tundra, muskeg, marshland and bogs, with vegetation and species proliferation steadily and rapidly increasing in variety and density, into taiga and then boreal forest in the south. It'll be slightly warmer than you'd expect for the latitude, because of thermal interaction with the Central Sea, and the mountain barrier against the cold north Atlantic air currents. Overall, it will be fairly reminiscent of Siberian arctic and sub-arctic zones.

Look over to the north east of our new Greenland - see a series of big islands. Likely not glaciated, not tall enough for snowcaps, and too evenly moderated by the Atlantic waters. Cold, wet, generally unpleasant. But likely supporting a healthy population of birds, and basking seals and sea mammals. It's the sort of place that people can live, thinly populated, intensely specialized for the environment, and largely left alone because no one else wants it.

The Western Drylands

Moseying on over to the west side, we don't have anything like that huge 10 degree of latitude mountain range that drives the biology and climate of the eastern side and contributes so much to the Central Sea. There is a small cluster of western coastal peaks in the southern half about 73 degrees latitude, which look like they'd go snowcap. Going by the map, they'd likely produce a fraction of the water and a smaller drainage basin than the eastern range. Most of their water contribution would probably go towards the lower parts of the Central Sea.

Overall, the west side is dryer. Still slightly warmer because of the Central Sea, but with more risk of cold air sweeping in. The weather is generally going to be more unpredictable, more storms, more snows.

Luckily, the west faces a small sea, known as Baffin Bay, a quarter of a million square miles in area, and is bordered by Ellesmere and Baffin Islands, so you're not going to have uninterrupted arctic savagery. The open ocean is a ferocious place, there's a lot of space for winds and storms to build up. But in the west, there isn't open ocean - geographical barriers slow things down. But it's still going to be colder and more volatile. The upside is that you'll see water coming in as precipitation, mostly winter snow. It will still be dryer, but not a desert.

This Tundra will be less productive, and it's not going to enrich nearly as quickly as you move south. Not until you get to that small mountain cluster midway down and its drainage basin, which goes to fairly productive taiga, and eventually, boreal forest. This will tend to resemble parts of the North American arctic, particularly the Yukon.

On the west side, between the coast and the Central Sea, there's a central elevated ... I wouldn't call it a ridge, maybe a highland or table lands, running north and south from which the landscape slopes downwards east and west, towards Baffin Bay on one side and the Central Sea on the other. This is different from the East side, where there's a continuous slope downwards from the mountains.

There will be subtle differences - on the western side towards the Atlantic, more precipitation, but more wind and lower temperatures. On the eastern side towards the Central Sea, dryer and warmer, but both sides productive in their own ways and on different timetables, with the central table land that runs down the middle of the west side being relatively barren.

The Southern Reaches

Okay, now let's take a jump south. What do we have in the southern quarter or fifth of the Island? Two coastal mountain ranges, an eastern range running almost due south, and a western range slouching towards the southeast, which meet in the southern tip, is almost looks like an arrowhead pointing south. These aren't as mighty or as impressive as the great eastern range. But some of many of them will snowcap, and we'll see a similar water dynamic, although with substantially less volume. So, a lot goes into the Atlantic. But given the morphology, you'll see a large volume of water, as much as half, flowing inland, north towards the Central Sea once again.

The southern geography is even more gently sloped than the eastern tundra side. And it's a long, long way to the south basin of the Central Sea. What you are going to get is very long, very slow meandering rivers and a lot of water deposition in the landscape, and a lot of silt and soil development. It will eventually drain into the Central Sea, but there's going to be a lot of evaporation, a lot of local water capture.

At the highest elevations in the south, you'll get mountain tundra. But as you proceed northwards towards the lower basin of the central sea, following the winding rivers, you'll notice a paradox. It will get warmer, apparently, as you go north. This is a factor of moving from mountains and highlands through increasingly lower elevations which will tend to be warmer and come further and further into the thermal regime surrounding the Central Sea.

What you'll find is scrub and shrub tundra, giving way to actual trees and taiga, and boreal forest, increasing in density and diversity. It's going to be crap trees - a lot of spruce, larch, poplar, maybe some aspen, stands of birch. The species distribution, tree population, and density is going to shift dramatically, depending on where you are, and may be dramatically different depending on which side of a hill you're on, or how close to a lake, or what the prevailing winds or elevation is.

There's going to be a lot of fairly marginal territory - a lot of places where a really bad winter or set of winters, a twenty year or fifty year event will just kill whole forests. But there'll be enough stable regions, that the forests will always recolonize. There'll be grasslands and savannah mixed in. You may see an evolving series of forest stages, scrublands and savannah, depending on the activities of animal populations, as well as climate and water fluctuations. But hey, you are going to have a lot of water, some decent warmth. So boreal forest extending up to the shores of the South Basin, and maybe the southern shores of the central basin.

In terms of the interior and boreal forest, mostly, it's not viable for grain, not even barley - maybe a few microclimates and sheltered zones here and there. You could probably grow vegetables in a number of places. There'd be lots of viable pasture for cattle, sheep, goats. It's also pretty hospitable for the indigenous big mammals, obviously.

The Great Central Sea

But where is all that water going? Look at the topographic map. It's all draining towards the center of Greenland, towards a vast Central Sea. And there are as many as three channels from the surrounding oceans, into that central sea - one in the Southeast, around Disko Bay, the other two in the Northwest and Northeast. In fact, some researchers have speculated that technically, Greenland should be considered three Islands, because of those channels.

What this gives us is an immense Central Sea in the heart of Greenland. On the topographic map, it's colored in blue to represent that it's at sea level, loosely divided into three basins, a large north, and smaller central and south basins. Assuming it's at sea level, or roughly equivalent to the surrounding ocean levels, it is immense.

Eyeballing the whole thing (including the southern lakes), I make it about 200,000, maybe 220,000 square miles. That beats the Caspian at 140,000 square miles, and the Black Sea at about 170,000 square miles.

It's not terribly deep. I'd say that the average depth, going by the topography, is probably about 200 to 250 feet. That's not much, compared to the Black sea and its average depth of 4000, and the Caspian's of 700. It still adds up to a lot of water, continuously being fed by the oceans, and the mountain drainage.

That's going to do a few things. First, all that extra water from the mountain drainages are going to raise the elevation. If there is ocean access, then it's going to tend towards the same sea level as the ocean. But during the summer, it's going to be continually fed by mountain ranges in the East, West and South. That's a lot of water, and so the Central Sea level will rise higher than the ocean.

That higher elevation is also probably going to mean the Central Sea cuts channels to the Atlantic Ocean, so there'll be some exchange. Now mostly, it's going to be the Central Sea flowing out into the Atlantic. But during winter, when the fresh water flow stops, the elevation may drop enough that there's occasional reverses, and the Atlantic flows into the Central Sea.

Most of the water will be coming in from the south; the Western mountains will drain into the southern part of the sea, the Southern mountains will drain towards the same basin. The Eastern mountain range runs almost the length of Greenland, but its northern rivers will thaw and run more slowly and for shorter periods than its more southerly rivers, so most of the Eastern water will be in the South.

That means that the south basins will tend to have the freshest water, the north the saltier water. Water from the south will tend to flow into the north basin in summer, and perhaps out to the ocean through the south-eastern channel.

When winter comes, the rivers, carrying water down from the mountains, freeze, the water inflow stops. At that point, you may even see currents reversing, with saltier water flowing from the north basin to the south, and out the south-western channel, until balance is reached. As I said, you may even see, depending on conditions, the winter flow reversing in the south-western channel to the ocean, with ocean waters flowing inland to the sea, though it's more likely the channel would eventually freeze.

What else can we say about the Central Sea? Variable salinity. All that fresh water coming in particularly from the south. We can expect the south basin especially, but also the central basin, and the eastern lip of the north basin along the mountain drainage basin to be significantly fresher than average. The south may act very much like a freshwater lake, particularly in the summer. And of course, salinity will be seasonal, as the influx of fresh water varies with the seasons.

You're probably going to get some significant thermal-regulation. Basically, it's about heat storage. Bodies of water, large bodies of water tend to moderate climate. In the interiors, far away from seas or oceans, temperature gets extreme - things get really hot in summer and during the days, and get really cold in winters and at nights. Near seas and oceans, bodies of water act as heat traps and flatten out temperatures, it doesn't get as cold in winter, it doesn't get as hot in summer.

That Central Sea is a really big volume of water, it's going to influence the thermal features of the landscape. Again, check the topography. Greenland is sort of a bowl, with the lake in the middle. That means that water will drain towards it. But it also means that air and wind will tend to flow towards it. Warm air rises, of course, so it's a bit more complicated. And while the glacial rivers will be slower and take more time to warm up, they may still be fairly cold. But the likelihood is that the geography is probably going to tend to transfer seasonal warmth towards the Central Sea. So, it's likely to be warmer waters than the arctic currents. That moderating effect will make the landscape on average a little warmer than it would normally be. It won't be huge, a few degrees at best. But when you're this far north, a few degrees can make a real difference in the quality of your tundra or taiga.

It's going to be an active sea. It's a narrow body of water stretching across ten degrees of latitude, so even small thermal differences will drive significant north/south currents. Throw in the contributions of major drainage from the south and east, variations in salinity - all of these are drivers for significant, stable seasonal currents. Despite currents, it's going to be a pretty calm sea, at least compared to the Atlantic, and especially so in the south. So, calm, steady, stable, predictable, seasonal. And of course, it will freeze over in the winter ... at those latitudes, everything does.

Let's get out our old chemistry textbook. Here's some interesting factoids about water, and about the ocean. Basically, life in the ocean, our fishy friends, survive by respirating dissolved oxygen in the water through their gills. I know that's painfully obvious. But when you think about it, one of the boundaries for sea life is the oceans, or the water's, capacity to carry dissolved oxygen. The more oxygen, the more fishies, or the bigger the fishies, they tend to go together, it's a food chain thing. The less oxygen, the fewer fishies.

Now, this isn't exactly rocket science. But let me throw in a couple of factoids. It seems that fresh water has a greater capacity of carrying dissolved oxygen than salt water. The fresher, the more oxy, the saltier, the less oxygen. That's why the Dead Sea is dead, too much salt crowding out the oxygen, fish can't breathe (or whatever it is called when you respirate through gills).

The next factoid: Cold water has a greater oxygen carrying capacity than warmer water. So, all those glacial streams entering the coastal Atlantic waters off Greenland are carrying and introducing a much higher dissolved oxygen content than the regular Atlantic waters. And the mixing of glacial fresh and Atlantic salt waters, the rapid currents coming off the glaciers are stirring up the sea bottom, producing turbidity and increasing the nutrient content of these waters. So, overall, good for fish, good for lots of fish, good for big fish and lots of them, and very good for sea mammals eating those fish.

Your Central Sea fishery is likely to be extremely productive. Maybe not as productive as the Grand Banks off Newfoundland, but maybe up there with or better than the Barents Sea or the Andean coasts.

For that matter, it's likely that the external ocean around Greenland's east and southern coasts will be extremely productive, fed as they are by fast moving glacial rivers rich with fresh water and oxygen, carrying nutrients down from the mountains, and stirring them up in their currents.

The Frigid Ocean Coasts

Now, just a few more observations - check the coastline. What do you see? Fjords. Lots of fjords. Which amount to sheltered bays, protected from the savage Atlantic winds, likely with freshwater drainage, and relatively stable though cold microclimates. Probably lots of good terrain for seal and walrus haul outs, and for sea birds. Good fishing, too.

In the south, below 70 degrees latitude, and preferably below 65 degrees latitude, you might have enough warmth and water for decent terrestrial vegetation in the fjords, shrubs and grasses. And in the very south, you'll probably see random stands of beaten up and puny looking birch and spruce trying to make a go of it.

You couldn't grow barley anywhere along the coast. I'm not saying you could have much of a go at it in the southern interior (maybe in a few spots, with the right microclimate). Up to 65 degrees latitude in the fjords, though, you might manage to grow a few vegetables.

Up to 70 degrees latitude, you might be able to pull enough pasture in your fjord to support a few goats and sheep, maybe even cattle ... if you invested heavily in protecting them from the elements and getting them through the winter. But I'll be honest, past 65 and the further you go, it would be a pretty hardscrabble life for Norse settlers, and only the fishery and sea mammal harvest would make it viable at all.

But you could manage it. It's not going to be uniform - you'll get an incredible amount of diversity in the fjords, depending on the latitude, the orientation, the height of surrounding lands, proximity to glacial waters, the adjacent ocean currents and winds, etc., everything from blasted heaths and barren rock lands to fairly nice garden spots next to each other. And it'll be tricky getting from one fjord to the next - overland travel will be intensely seasonal, and erratic, and some places will be inaccessible all year round, other places only accessible to specific other places.

Of course, coastal peoples would also be making a go of it, with a lower population density, more dependence on sea protein, and a seasonal subsistence basket.

Let's take another look at the topographic map on your cover and the Eastern mountain ranges. We'll notice on the Atlantic side, that curve is steep. It's a downhill slalom. The water moves damned fast and at velocity into the ocean. Good for turbidity and coastal currents that stir up the bottom. Fair enough, most of the water depositing is forming on that side, so it's good that it's moving out fast.

Turbidity, silt and mountain run off, and injections of fresh oxygenated water in the summers will make the coastal waters off Greenland very rich and biologically productive. So, you'll get a very productive fishery, lots of fish, lots of sea mammals.

Breaching the Interior

One interesting thing, looking at this topographic map, is that the interior is going to be pretty inaccessible from the coasts. Greenland is going to be hard to get into.

Most places out there, we have rivers draining their way out from continental interiors towards the open sea or ocean - the Nile, the Amazon, the Yellow, the Ganges, the Mississippi, the Rhine, the Danube, yadda yadda. All you have to do is sail along the coasts till you come to them, start sailing up them, and voila, you're in the interior.

Not this version of Greenland. Most of the drainage of Greenland's rivers, particularly the navigable rivers, is from the highlands and mountains to the interior Central Sea, not the coasts. There are coastal rivers of course, coming down from the mountains and highlands and emptying into the Ocean. But they're short and fast moving, mostly not all that navigable, and they generally don't connect to any of the interior water complexes. So, you'd have to do a lot of really hard climbing up and down mountains and portaging through mountain passes an unreasonable distance to try and get towards the interior river systems. I'm not saying it's impossible, I'm just saying it can't be done. The interior is going to be extremely, unreasonably difficult to access from most of the coast.

Not entirely impossible. On the east coast, there's a stretch of a couple of hundred miles around latitude 65, between the Eastern and the South Eastern mountain complexes, where the hill country looks like it might be low enough and broken up enough that you could maybe find some pathways to the interior. Maybe. Particularly if you're ready to do a lot of walking. It's not easy, but at least you're not climbing over mountains.

On the western coasts, between latitude 66 and 70, you might have better luck finding pathways to the interior, but mostly again, this will involve a lot of walking. However, if we look closely, there is, next to the western edge of the southern basin, a series of lakes and bays. Now on the topographic map, they're not connected at sea level. But it's likely that the southern basin is elevated above sea level, so there's a good chance that here you might have an access channel to the Atlantic Ocean. Maybe that's a navigable waterway, or maybe it's a nonstop series of hellish waterfalls and rapids.

But note the presence of a fairly big mountainous island and peninsula immediately to the north - likely snowcapped, and potentially calving small icebergs or discharging fresh water - these are likely to produce unpredictable and unpleasant local winds and currents. Nothing that can't be handled, but not inviting.

Of course, there may be a couple of sea accesses in the far north, but you're up around 75 or 80 degrees latitude. It's not practical or viable as a gateway. Those sea accesses would probably be frozen for three quarters of the year.

There are gaps in the mountain and highland ranges, particularly on the east coast, around a place near Disko Bay, which, depending on elevation, might give inflow or outflow from the surrounding saltwater oceans to the interior lowland.

Flora and Fauna in Alternate Greenland

So, what's our picture of Greenland? Starting in the north, rocky frozen tundra, in the mountains and highlands, the landscape won't be too different, mountain elevations and snow caps mean colder temperatures and climate year-round. But as we move south, the landscape starts to change. The vegetation gets thicker, the soil more productive. Rivers and marshes proliferate along the lowlands sloping towards the central sea, with the eastern flatlands being wetter and richer, the western flatlands being dryer. The further south we go, the more trees and brush we see, more small lakes, eventually transitioning to full boreal forest in the southern quarter. What's living there?

Let's start with the Central Sea. There's likely contact between the Atlantic Ocean and the Central Sea, outflow, possibly inflow. Biologically, we can assume that it's heavily influenced by north Atlantic Ocean flora and fauna. Kelp, algae, fish species - arctic char, salmon, cod, all the way up to Greenland sharks - there's pathways for entry. The variable salinity will mean that a lot of the saltwater species are going to evolve varying degrees of tolerance, all the way up to freshwater adaptation. They may colonize freshwater niches. You may also see, particularly in the south and east, freshwater species, perhaps fairly archaic ones - including big sturgeon.

It's going to be an extremely productive sea biologically, particularly the south and central basins. You know the recipe - cold waters and fresh waters carry more oxygen, which translates to more biological productivity, shallow basin allows for more turbidity from the sea floor, releasing nutrients, and of course, the drainage from the rivers and lakes are carrying silt and sediments, which are also contributing nutrients. As I said, basically, this is a crazy productive sea, particularly in the south basin. We're talking Barents and Andean shore levels of productivity, and a wide, diverse and very active biology, with a lot of lively biomass.

You'll probably get marine mammals. Seals, certainly, particularly the arctic seals. Porpoises range extends around the waters of Greenland, so we might see them. Orca may or may not end up there, although that seems unlikely. Baleen whales like the Bowhead may be a long shot. If there is a local population, it's likely a dwarf form of Bowhead.

Belugas are very tolerant to fresh water and are often found in rivers. Their natural range includes the coastal waters west of Greenland. They could likely get in there. Would they survive? That depends on the extent or degree to which the Central Sea freezes in the winter - if the whole sea freezes, then they may not be able to find breathing spaces through the ice. Freezing is a problem, some seals have claws to help them scrape holes through the ice, Bowhead whales have reinforced skulls to break through. Belugas not so much. On the other hand, if the lower basins don't quite freeze solid in the winter, or the winter currents keep the ice breaking up, then the Belugas might make a go of it, seasonally migrating around the Sea.

Remember I said walrus? Walrus are benthic (bottom) feeders, they basically travel around the sea floor, at depths of up to 250 feet, using their whiskers and tusks to stir up sediment and feel around, and then hovering up mollusks with vacuum suction - because of their activity on the sea floor, they're considered a pyramid species, liberating and stirring sediments and nutrients which then support an assortment of feeder species and charge up the ecology. And this sea is spectacular walrus habitat, it's practically made for them. The central sea would be perfect walrus territory, so you could expect a dense population of Walrus, and if the theory is correct, a turbo-charge to the biological productivity.

Walrus have not done well in the human era. Their bones have been found as far south as the St. Lawrence in Canada, and in Scotland and Scandinavia in Europe. Unfortunately, their need to occasionally haul themselves out of the water, and their slow reproduction has resulted in extinction over much of their range due to overhunting.

One sea mammal you won't get are sea cows. Sadly, Steller's Sea Cow is native to the pacific only, on the other side of North America - no way for them to get from there to here.

The other Sirenians are strictly tropical. That's a shame, because there's an empty niche for something like them.

You're likely to see large colonies of opportunistic seabirds, from seagulls and puffin to fish eagles. You'll also expect a good population of shoreline feeders, most likely polar bears, possibly brown bears, or speciated polar bears. Wolves. Not sure about otters, but even if we don't get otters, it's likely that some other mustelid will move towards that niche. If any herbivore can manage salt tolerance, there's likely rich kelp beds.

What about land animals? Now that could get really interesting. At a minimum ,you might see Greenland colonized by the modern standard repertoire of arctic and sub-arctic megafauna: Caribou, Musk Ox, Polar Bears, Wolves ... possibly Moose, maybe even Bison or Beavers, big Cats, or some additional variety of Bear. You might even get some specially adapted Greenland varieties, such as Polar Bear who have shifted back to being land predators, or Moose who got salt tolerant to take advantage of seagrasses.

Mammoths, Camels and Sloths

Or, depending, we could get a little more exotic. How about Mammoths? We know that the Wooly Mammoths were active in both Siberia and North America. Obviously, they were crossing back and forth over the Bering Strait. So, they were up and about in the region.

Now, there's no indication that Woolly Mammoths inhabited the eastern Canadian Arctic or Arctic Islands or ever got to Greenland. We don't have any fossil record of Wooly Mammoths on Baffin Island, or Ellesmere which is next to Greenland. But we do have fossil forests on Ellesmere Island, and other extinct large animals. If Mammoths could cross the

Bering Strait, it's likely that they could have made it across the narrow spaces to Ellesmere, and from there, Greenland. It's a long shot, but maybe.

Is there enough space in this Greenland for a population of Wooly Mammoths? A dwarf population survived on Wrangel Island for at least six thousand years, and Wrangel is only 4000 square miles. Greenland is 830,000 square miles. On the other hand, 830,000 is pretty good, but it's not Eurasia or even North America.

But not all of that 830,000 is Mammoth habitat. Let's break it down. Of that 830,000 miles, let's assume about 20% - 166,000 square miles - is Arctic desert in the north. Mammoths aren't good swimmers, so let's knock off another 20%, roughly 166,000 square miles for the Central Sea and its waterways. Mammoths aren't really mountain climbers, so let's discount another 20% or 166,000 square miles.

That leaves about 332,000 square miles for Mammoths. About the size of France and Germany together. That's everything from subarctic muskeg, to marsh, to taiga and boreal forest. Everything from no quality, to low quality, to high quality Mammoth territory. Let's say no quality/low quality habitat is two thirds, It's still Greenland. You've got maybe 111,000 square miles of prime Mammoth country. Let's cut that in half, call it 55,000 square miles.

That would still be twice the size Sri Lanka, and it's got a healthy population of Indian Elephants. But then, Sri Lanka is tropical, lots more biomass year-round, lots more energy. On the other hand, only a fraction of Sri Lanka, 20% or less, say 5000 square miles is Elephant habitat. So, Greenland seems to have at least ten times that. Lots of room for a Mammoth population.

So ... let's assume that Mammoth territory extended from Boreal forest to Shrub Tundra. With Shrub Tundra being shitty, low density, so thin the ribs are showing, but survivable mammoth territory, and boreal forest being buffet land. And let's assume that they're not taking up the entirety but sharing the vegetation with a bunch of other species, so they're probably actually taking up 15 to 20% of the available food. And let's assume that given the latitudes and stuff, that the regular elephants in Africa and India need a fraction of the territory 'cause it's so warm and productive and can have at least two or three times the population density ...

What's the likely mammoth population? Apparently, you can find anything on the internet, someone actually calculated population densities for Woolly Mammoths. They are considered to have population densities from 0.1 to 4 individuals per square kilometer. Let's assume a relatively low density of 0.3 to 0.5. 50,000 square miles translates to 130,000 square kilometers - gives us roughly between 40,000 and 65,000 animals. Those are pretty big herds. Even assuming half those numbers, that's a healthy population. Greenland is smaller than their native range, so you've probably got smaller Mammoths over time - but something between 80% or 50% of their original size would still be impressive.

In our history, after hundreds of thousands of years, Mammoths died out about 10,000 years ago. A relic population survived until 4000 years ago. That's amazing. Literally, the final Mammoths died off at the same time as the pyramids were being built. They survived until the time frame of human civilization! Those Mammoths were a small relic population on Wrangel Island, that managed to survive because there were no humans to hunt them.

But the thing with Greenland, it wasn't even discovered by humans until about 4500 years ago, and those humans would have found two or three robust populations of mammoths, on the East, West and South of the Central Sea. What this means is that Mammoths might have survived in Greenland longer, perhaps for thousands of years into historical times. Possibly long enough that the Vikings might have encountered them. Or even to the present. The thought of Mammoths surviving into the 19th or 20th century is ... fun.

There are other possible exotic animals in Greenland. Not the Woolly Rhino, unfortunately. They never made it into North America. But other animals passed back and forth between North America and Asia, and were clearly operating at high latitudes and in the broad vicinity. Some of them might have made it into Greenland.

One possibility are sloths. Megalonyx was a bear-sized, flat-footed sloth, ranging up to nine feet long and weighing up to two thousand pound, whose range extended as far as Alaska and the Yukon, which survived into the Holocene, roughly eleven thousand years ago, and was definitely hunted by humans. I do think it's a stretch to get Megalonyx up as far as Ellesmere and into Greenland.

Depending on time frame, whether Greenland never glaciated, never completely glaciated, or de-glaciated, it's possible that other animals that inhabited the arctic in the last few million years might have ended up in Greenland.

Tapirs, for instance, although they're now native to tropical regions in both South America and Asia. The Cloud Tapir finds itself at home in the Andean mountains and is very tolerant of sub-zero temperatures. Ancestral Tapirs must have travelled across the Bering Strait. Had they managed to find our Greenland, the Central Sea and the lakes, rivers and marshes would have been prime habitat. It seems counterintuitive to find such animals here, but species often end up in strange places.

An excellent candidate would have been descendants of Paracamelus, including the High Arctic Camel, and the Yukon Giant Camel. Paracamelus fossils have actually been found on Ellesmere Island, which is just a skip away from Greenland. Camels originated in North America, of course, before moving to South America, where they evolved into Andean Llamas and Alpacas, and crossed the Bering Strait for the varieties that we know today.

One really interesting thing about Camels is their utter ruggedness. They could adapt to be quite at home in the foothills and mountain ranges of Greenland, as the Llamas are in the Andes. One interesting species, the Wild Bactrian Camel, is actually able to subsist on water even saltier than seawater, which is astounding

Remember how I mentioned the likelihood that the shallows of the Central Sea would be fertile territory for seaweeds and sea grasses, but there were no sea cows to eat them? That was an empty niche. Well, hypothetically, you could have Moose, or Tapirs or Camels evolving to occupy that niche, all they'd really need would be adaptations to water, and salinity tolerance. Moose and Tapir are already water adapted, and Camels are salt tolerant, take your pick.

But is there a point? Assuming our hypothetical Greenland really was a Lost World, a refuge for extinct megafauna, wouldn't they just go extinct anyway when humans show up? By the modern era, wouldn't we be back to caribou, musk ox and polar bears?

If humans show up in 2500 BC, how much longer would Mammoths and other megafauna have survived? The North American experience seems to suggest humans co-existed with megafauna for twenty or thirty thousand years before the megafauna went extinct ten thousand years ago. So, either a particularly gifted big game hunting culture came along, or some kind of ecological bottleneck hit that tipped the balance.

The Fall of Atlantis – Page 137

There's some evidence that humans were on Madagascar foraging as far back as 2000 years ago, although this is controversial. The mass extinctions of megafauna seem to have spread out around 1000 to as recently as 500 CE. So, there's at least a few hundred years of overlap. They didn't all get wiped out at once. In the Madagascar case, the megafauna's extinctions came at least in part to habitat modification by human action, particularly fires and fire management.

As I modeled out the cultures invading Greenland, they seemed to consistently be coastal cultures whose lives revolved around harvesting sea protein, particularly sea mammals in what would still be a very difficult landscape, which orients towards conservative stable societies. Which means that their tool kits would not be well adapted to hunting megafauna, they'd probably be very slow to colonize the interior away from coasts, and they're unlikely to radically transform the landscape in ways that spelled doom in other areas. And large parts of it are simply a harsh landscape for humans. So perhaps survival to modern times wouldn't be out of the question.

In the end, it's a matter of speculation and choice, as to what this Greenland could be like - we could populate it with a standard suite of Arctic and Sub-Arctic fauna. Or we could turn it into a veritable lost world with mammoths, mountain camels and herds of a seaweed munching salt tolerant herbivore species.

Old Greenland, The Peoples

In our real history, Greenland probably is in the running for the most inhospitable place on Earth. Antarctica wins. But Greenland? It's definitely up there. That's saying something.

Humans are an adaptable species. We go everywhere, we manage to find a way to make a living anywhere. Between 60,000 and 10,000 years ago, humans had colonized most of the planet - by that time, we'd found Indonesia, the Philippines, Australia, North and South America. Basically, the only places we hadn't reached - Madagascar, New Zealand, Iceland, Antarctica, Greenland, were either incredibly hard to reach, or incredibly difficult to live in.

Humans crossed the Bering Strait several times. The earliest colonists may have gone as far back as 40,000 years ago. They immediately headed south; their traces have been found in South America. They don't seem to have done much damage, though.

That's the first thing, early humans overran every other bit of two continents, but when they looked to Greenland, it was 30,000 years of 'nope.'

Then about 10,000 years ago, a new set of colonists, these were big game hunters came through. And that's where you got the big mass extinctions all over North and South America. But they headed south, too. It seems that none of our early ancestors wanted to live in the Canadian Arctic or try Greenland. Almost anywhere but there.

Another 6000 years of 'nope' to Greenland.

Humans had managed to find and settle just about every remaining piece of real estate, short of Antarctica. We'd found the Azores, the Canaries, the Cape Verdes and Caribbean in the Atlantic, we found just about every Island worth having in the Pacific, including Hawaii, Rapa Nui and the Aleutians. We'd found Tierra del Fuego, Madagascar, Iceland and New Zealand, and we made a go of all those places.

But Greenland? Greenland was where humanity failed. And failed four times in a row. Greenland's history is unique in that it's been settled five times, by five different human cultures, including the Norse and the Inuit, and four of those attempts failed. Only the Inuit managed to stick. And even there, they find barrows where Inuit communities slowly starved to death in their homes during hard times.

That's not surprising, given that the place is a giant Island bigger than Mexico under a two mile thick glacier, with only a narrow ring of inhospitable tundra around it.

Greenland's first inhabitants were the Saqqaq culture, also called paleo-eskimos. That's not what they called themselves, but they're gone so we had to call them something. They showed up in Greenland about 2500 BCE, and they lasted until about 800 BCE before vanishing. From the remains, we know that they're related to the Chukchi and Koryak of Siberia. So, they must have been the descendants of a people who came over from Siberia and somehow spread across Alaska and Northern Canada before reaching Greenland. But those intermediate steps seem to be lost to us. The Inuit, a separate people, also seem to have crossed over from Siberia in that time frame, but ended up staying parked in Alaska until about a thousand years ago.

The Saqqaq lived in small tents, used bows and arrows, and lived off sea mammals, seals and walrus mostly. It's not clear whether they used boats at all or had simply marched across the ice floes. Although dogs came with them, showing up around 2000 BC they didn't seem to use dogsleds. They used stone tools, obviously, but halfway through their era, they started working sandstone.

We don't really know what happened to them. Best guess is that times just got tough - Greenland went through a long cold spell, or maybe the currents shifted enough that the sea mammals weren't as easy to catch. They vanished.

Around the same time, there was another human culture that made it into Greenland. This group, though, clung to the northern part of Greenland, which was a polar desert. They didn't move south, so odds are that the Saqqaq weren't welcoming. Instead, they were stuck with the worst part of Greenland. These precarious survivors were called the 'Independence I' culture, and survived from about 2400 BCE to 1300 BCE before vanishing.

Several hundred years later, another group showed up, 'Independence II,' living in the same northern region for about 600 years, from roughly 700 BCE to 100 BCE. The Independence II culture occupied a territory the size of a European country, but they may have amounted to only a handful of families - a couple of hundred people if that, which illustrates how utterly barren their landscape was.

Next came the Dorset. The early Dorset appeared around 700 BCE, long after the Saqqaq had died off, and lasted until about 1 BCE. And then they disappeared. Greenland seems to have been utterly abandoned for most of the early Christian era.

Then, later, Dorset showed up in Greenland seven hundred years later, around 700 CE and lasted until about 1300 CE before disappearing again. Peculiarly, unlike either the earlier Saqqaq and the later Inuit, the Dorset seemed to lack bows and arrows, or drills. It's not clear, but they seem to have had skin boats, and appear to have lacked dogsleds. Their technology was built around their harpoons. Perhaps these deficits limited their expansion and confined them to northern Greenland.

Meanwhile, in the south, the Norse showed up about 1000 CE. There's some indication that the Greenland Norse may have traded with the Canadian Dorset on Baffin Island. But on Greenland, the Norse stayed in the south, don't seem to have ever met the Dorset who clung to the north. The Norse only barely outlasted the Dorset, clinging on till about 1450 CE.

Around the time the Dorset were disappearing, the Thule were showing up - the people who would be known as Inuit. Eventually, they'd be the last people standing.

It's not clear what was going on with them. For two thousand years, the Thule had parked in Alaska, doing nothing much. And through a lot of this time, the Dorset were the dominant ethnic group across the north. Then suddenly, the Dorset seemed to collapse - this seems to coincide with the Medieval Warm period, so it may be that their lifestyle couldn't cope with climate change. Instead, the Norse exploded across the north as far as Greenland and Labrador. Dogsleds and skin boats allowed them to travel faster and further.

So this is the history of Greenland. Desperate cultures clinging to marginal existences in parts of Greenland, making a go of it for a few hundred years, and withering away.

A New Path for Greenland's Peoples

Well, this Greenland is a lot friendlier place. Flat out, there's just a huge amount of unglaciated territory in comparison. And the landscape is biologically richer, especially towards the south. There's much more diversity of landscapes, different zones of tundra, desert tundra, dry tundra, wet tundra, shrub tundra, taiga, boreal forest, freshwater lakes and rivers, seas and oceans.

But it's not any easier to reach. Greenland is mostly surrounded by cold, raging inhospitable oceans. It's not easy to cross hundreds of miles of arctic and Sub-arctic Ocean. That technology wouldn't exist until the Vikings around 1000 AD.

It's possible to get to Greenland, but not easy. What you have to do is travel through the Canadian arctic, Island after Island, until you get to Ellesmere, the northernmost Island. Then you have to go to the far north of Ellesmere, approximately 80 or 83 north, within 10 degrees latitude of the North Pole. There you'll find a channel between Greenland and Ellesmere, a few hundred miles long, ranging from 11 to over 100 miles wide. Now, if you're lucky, you're going in winter, the current isn't too bad, and the ice has frozen. You can walk there ... into northern Greenland, which is an arctic desert. It gets a lot nicer further south, but you've got to pass through the toughest parts first.

So, in this version of history, humans don't find Greenland any earlier than they do in our history. It's just that hard. What we'll see is the same suite of suitors - the Saqqaq, the Independence I and II, the old Dorset, the new Dorset, the Norse and the Thule/Inuit.

But this is a nicer, kinder Greenland. What this means is that the successive cultures probably aren't as marginal, and they don't go extinct. At least, not naturally. Rather, they're much more likely to expand, and to adapt to different regions.

So let's chart them out. We'll assume a butterfly net, and we'll assume that Greenland not being glaciated changes no ocean currents, no wind patterns, the rest of the world simply goes on its merry way, with the same people being born and dying.

The Saqqaq - 2400 to 1600 BC

The first visitors, once again, are the Saqqaq. In our history, their culture seems to have centered around Disko Bay, about halfway down the western side of Greenland. Disko Bay was pretty sheltered and a rich hunting ground for walrus and seal - both the Inuit and the Norse travelled there to hunt. For the Saqqaq to get to Disko Bay, it means that they had to come in from the north, from Ellesmere, and travel down the Western coast. So that's how they come in, in this new history.

The Independence I culture, must have come later, since they travelled further along the northern shore. Otherwise, they would have headed south, unless the Saqqaq were already there. Basically, Independence I were stuck with the leftovers that the Saqqaq had abandoned.

So in universe, the Saqqaq had come across from Ellesmere. Once again, the northern part of Greenland is very much like our timeline - an arctic desert. The Saqqaq abandon it, heading south. In our timeline, the only thing they could do was follow the coast. In this timeline, they disperse south, some following the coast, but others go inland, where they come to the shores of the Central Sea, and split, moving down the eastern and western Central Sea coastlines.

Now, the Saqqaq lack dogsleds, and perhaps boats, so they have serious mobility issues. It's hard to move far, it's hard to carry a lot. They're probably going to stick close to the coastlines and water bodies, where they can harvest walrus and seal, catch fish in spawning season, or with ice fishing. But mobility issues mean that it's likely difficult to exploit the inlands - sure there's game there, but it's harder to get to, doesn't come to where you're waiting, is prone to running away, and when you kill it, you're going to have to schlep it. So, the Inlands will tend to be thinly populated.

The Saqqaq diverge into three coastal tribes, Ocean Coast along the west coast, Central Sea East Coast, and Central Sea

West Coast. All very similar, but physically, mostly out of touch with each other, and with enough significant differences in resources that the cultures will diverge. They're also likely to move relatively slowly - the founding populations are small, perhaps only a handful of family groups, it will take time to grow. The Saqqaq cultures are probably going to take at least four or five hundred years to reach and begin populating the south and central basins. And probably a couple of hundred more years to populate the southern reaches.

Following on the Saqqaq will be the Independence 1 culture. The history will be similar. They'll cross over from Ellesmere. The south will already be occupied by the Saqqaq, and so the Independence I will travel east, crossing and occupying the northern polar desert. It's a harsh life, but still slightly more generous than our universe, and there are southern resources to plunder, if you can sneak past or fight the Saqqaq, or bypass them. You'll see small groups of Independence 1 infiltrating the highlands and mountains of both the east and west, living on Caribou and Arctic hare, while the Saqqaq prefer the richer coastal regions. But there's a limit to how far south they can penetrate - the further south we go, the more tolerable the Tundra becomes, and the more the Saqqaq are inclined to expand into it. Independence 1 infiltration stops about halfway down the north basin, about latitude 75.

The Independence Culture also follows the western coasts, settling on the coastal islands and peninsulas in the shadows of the glaciers. These isolated populations diverge strongly, becoming rather distinct from other Independence 1 groups.

This phase covers the first eight hundred years, give or take. From 2400 BC to 1600 BC. Human presence is thin, particularly in the uplands. Dogs are late arrivals, around 2000 BC, and they don't seem to be used for much. There's very little pressure on the local flora and fauna. Most of the harvest is sea based, and while the land animals are hunted, they're not primary game.

The Saqqaq- 1600 to 800 BC

The East and West Coast tribes of the Central Sea reach, and within a century or two of each other at the most, begin to colonize the shores of the southern basin. By this time, the cultures have diverged strongly, but their dialects are still roughly intelligible to each other. Initially, the groups are civil when they encounter each other. There's enough space and enough sustenance for everyone, and everyone can talk to each other. We see the beginning of ceremonial greetings and exchanges, which slowly evolve into formal trade networks, stretching up the coast.

The Ocean Coast people have moved south as well, finding and spreading up the southwestern channel to the Interior, which brings them into contact with the Central Sea tribes. They have also found telluric Iron from Disko Bay and meteoric Iron from Cape Hope, a significant edge in hunting, war and trading, which makes up for their otherwise thinner and more hardscrabble population. The eastern and western sea coasters have enough difference in their environments, in medicinal plants, stone etc., that trade works. The trade networks stretch up the three coastlines, with ceremonial and practical goods slowly moving back and forth.

In the north, Saqqaq at the far ends of the trading circuit, now acquainted with the idea of exchange, even begin trading with the Inland and northern Independence I. It's not all ponies, however. The slowly expanding northern Saqqaq are impinging steadily on the inland Independence people, who have little choice but to withdraw. The result is often brushfire conflicts and raids. Trade up there becomes very formal, only at certain times, certain places, everyone shows up with their posse, everyone is armed with their hands on their weapons.

Around the Southern Basin, things are really starting to heat up, though. Over the centuries, the population density of the Southern and Central basins increases. Frictions increase between founding populations, and intermittent raiding emerges alongside trading. But more important things are happening. The landscape around the Southern and Central basins is extremely productive, supporting an increasingly robust population. But it's also very different environment, with taiga and boreal forest, and a density of woodland species. There are different and new opportunities, inviting new words, new technology. From different starting points, the three coastal tribes adapt and evolve, sometimes borrowing words and techniques from each other, sometimes independently inventing, sometimes competing with and refining each other's inventions.

The south and central basin Saqqaq evolve into a fourth Saqqaq culture, albeit a feuding and fractious one, with many local subcultures. Intermittent war and conflict makes them territorial. Competition and exchange of ideas, ceremonial and trade occasions drive an increasingly sophisticated culture, with several developing artistic traditions, including heavy cultural investment in the production of ceremonial and trade objects, and the creation of petroforms, landmarks and even forts to mark and protect territories. Eventually, towards the end of Phase 2, we will start to see local projects such as fish traps, dams, and crude rafts. No permanent or semi-permanent settlements yet, however. The populations are too dependent on sea mammals, particularly walrus, which suffer local depletions.

Conflict between these groups sometimes results in some of them being pushed out of the basin regions, forced to eke out a living with their woodland skills in the southern boreal forests. This becomes a fifth group, denied the traditional sustenance of sea protein, they survive as small, nomadic woodland hunters. This is the first Saqqaq culture to specialize in land animals. The Sea Basin Saqqaq consider them savages and cannibals. Although they occupy the lowland boreal forest, they generally avoid the less productive and less desirable highlands.

Meanwhile, the Atlantic Coast Saqqaq continue to move south. The western mountain range prevents them from moving inland. Instead, they occupy coastal fjords, jumping or climbing along shores or valleys from one to another, forming diverging microcultures.

Arrival of the Dorset - 800 BC to 1 BC

So what are we up to at this point? Most of Greenland now has been colonized by two ethnic/cultural groups, the Saqqaq and Independence I. Mostly dominated by the Saqqaq. But over 1600 years, both groups have differentiated into some fairly distinctive cultures or subcultures. There are still large parts of Greenland that are unoccupied - primarily the central and southern East Atlantic coastal fjords, and the Southern highlands, and while the interior tundra is inhabited, the population is extremely thin. Most of the population is clustering along the coasts, both inner and outer, and only around the southern basin are you seeing anything like density or social complexity building up.

For the most part, the human presence hasn't affected Greenland at all. The Central Sea is rich enough and productive enough that humans haven't made much of a dent in the harvest. Only in the south basin are there transient local depletions of sea mammals, walrus and seals, and these pass quickly as the local people move elsewhere and neighboring sea mammals move into depleted territory and repopulate. Land animals aren't much bothered. The interior population densities are so low that the great herds of caribou and musk ox, camel and mammoth barely notice the presence of humans. They're well used to the occasionally biped polar bears, so they're already half wary of these strangers and harder to hunt. Mostly, they get left alone.

All else being equal, we could just let the whole place sit for another several thousand years and not expect too much - maybe a steady gradual rise in population density - but never beyond hunter gatherer levels, and population crashes every now and then when the bad weather hits or some other threshold is reached. Maybe the gradual extinction of some of the more vulnerable species. But no reason to expect anything dramatic.

All else is not equal, because the third culture is going to be arriving. This is when the Dorset come to visit.

Now the Dorset are an interesting folk. We don't know a lot about them. The Inuit described them as giants, extraordinarily strong, but rather timid, a people that could wring the neck of a walrus but be driven away by a shout. They lacked bows and arrows, and bowstring drills. But they did have sophisticated toggle harpoons. They seemed to have had yarn. They had kayaks, but no umiaks (big skin boats capable of carrying whole families and cargo). They had sleds, but not dogsleds. They lived in igloos. They seemed to have been well suited to their environment, their toolkit was overall superior to and more specialized than the preceding cultures.

In our time, of course, the Dorset walked into an empty Greenland, and mostly stayed in the upper regions where their toolkit worked best. In this history, the Dorset encounter two existing populations, both of which are doing relatively well.

It's possible that nothing happens. The Dorset cross over from Ellesmere, take a look around, are met by the occupants, and come back the way they came. Which isn't much fun. It's certainly possible. For interpersonal tribal conflicts bows and arrows are a lot handier than harpoons. Whatever their skill sets, it's hard to invade someone else's territory and make it stick.

Hard, but not impossible. The Dorset invasions are more erratic in this history and more nuanced. The indigenous populations of Independence and Saqqaq are making a living on their coasts and tundra. But this is very marginal territory, and a sharp change in weather for a few years can bring disaster. And that's happened again and again. When you're passing time by centuries, a four or five year, or a decade long spell of unusually savage cold or disruptive warmth is almost common. When this happens, the local populations will try to adapt, to shift their subsistence basket. But if they can't, if the disruption is too great, then the only thing the population can do is collapse. Not all of them, there'll be survivors, places where for one reason or another disaster bypasses. And when good times come around again, they'll repopulate what has been abandoned.

Except here in the third phase, during these periodic disaster seasons, the Dorset come in, surviving and thriving on a much better, more effective, coastal survival package. They settle, they spread, and eventually, they stop as climate stabilizes and the Saqqaq expand. But the Dorset remain in the territories they've settled. And when the next round of disruptive climate comes along, which brings a retreat or collapse of the Saqqaq and Independence folk, the Dorset expand again.

Over the next few centuries, the Dorset expand steadily, moving down the western Atlantic coast of Greenland, eventually almost completely displacing the Saqqaq. The Saqqaq aren't driven entirely from the region. They survive in coastal pockets. And by the time the Dorset reach Disko Bay, they've reached the natural limits of their expansion - past that point, the Saqqaq are much too well established and too dense to be displaced.

In the north, they move across the Arctic Ocean coast, pushing the Independence culture east and south. Eventually, the Independence 1 are left only with the northeastern corner of Greenland, and their Islands. On the other hand, the collapse of the Saqqaq in the face of the Dorset leaves the thinly populated Tundra interior even more thinly populated in the north and west, so the scattered hunter gatherers of Independence abandon the sea and become an inland peoples.

As to the Central Sea, the Dorset barely make an impact. The climate around the Central Sea is simply too consistent and stable. It's less prone to the savage oscillations driven in from the Atlantic and it tends to moderate. Saqqaq collapses are fewer and far less intense. A tributary of the Dorset occupy slivers of the northern interior coastline. But mostly, the Central Sea is a Saqqaq lake, and the Dorset are eventually merged and become a mixed population there.

The introduction of the Dorset isn't as violent as you might think. Yes, there's some raiding, some burning, some killing and kidnapping. But the Dorset expansions aren't warlike, but a matter of simply being more efficient. Not that efficiency counts for much in good times. But in bad times, it means you survive when your neighbors don't, that you expand where they've retreated. In circumstances like that, hard times, you learn to be good neighbors. Saqqaq wives and children are adopted into Dorset families, sometimes there's begging or voluntary servitude. There's communication and trade. Life is hard, no one needs to fight.

The result is over time, a trickle of cultural exchange. Not just ceremonial and religious objects, trade goods. But loan words make it back and forth. The Dorset pick up bows and drills, and this enhances their ability to harvest and spin yarn. Igloos, Kayaks and toggle harpoons transmit slowly through Greenland. This doesn't happen right away, and it doesn't transmit rapidly. One of the things you have to understand about cultures in a landscape this harsh and barren is that innovation is not a welcome thing.

The land is unforgiving, what works, works. New things usually get you killed - innovation is unnecessary risks, missed meals, lost game, opportunities squandered. You stick with what worked for your father and grandfather, mother and grandmother, because it worked and you can rely on it.

So if it takes hundreds of years for the Dorset to truly dominate their parts of Greenland, it takes more hundreds of years for their innovations to spread widely. It's only toward the end of the third phase that Kayaks and Toggle harpoons really make it to the Southern basin.

And that is the third Phase, from about 800 BCE extending to the Common Era.

Fusion and Interchange - 1 CE to 700 - CE

The fourth phase of Greenland's ethnographic and cultural evolution we will consider having run from approximately 1 CE to 1200 CE, concluding with contact from the Norse and Inuit, in the north and south. Largely, this was a period without major changes, marked in most cases by a slow but gradual increase in population and in subsistence tool kits.

Despite this, there were significant developments. Sometime around 600 CE, there was a second wave of Dorset immigration. This secondary wave established themselves in the north, partially displacing the Independence 1 culture, and their own Dorset predecessors. This seems to have produced a marked pulse of Dorset artifacts, tools and techniques through the rest of Greenland.

In particular, Independence 1 culture was heavily influenced by the Dorset, to the point of transformation, and is referred to as Independence 2. Kayaks became particularly important, especially to the Island cultures.

Along the southern coasts, the kayak and variations thereof became a boon to the Atlantic Coast Saqqaq and accelerated their colonization of southern fjords. Between about 400 and 700 CE, the Atlantic Saqqaq rounded the southern cape and proceeded up Greenland's eastern coast, falling just short of encountering the Independence Island populations. More significantly, the kayak allowed the coastal Saqqaq to communicate and interact more dynamically.

Local trading arrangements began to knit together into a trading network which encompassed most of the populations and ethnicities on the island. Obsidian from the far northern islands made their way to the coastal settlements in the south. Ivory, amber, herbs and ceremonial objects travelled hundreds of miles. Most of this trade was in extremely small volumes. But the south and central basin became a magnet for trade goods.

A major trade good was telluric iron from Disko Bay. However, sometime around 300 / 600 CE, copper deposits were found by Saqqaq in the eastern highlands, in the form of place deposits washed down by glacial rivers. At first, these were simply used locally. But copper artifacts were found in the south basin as early as 700. And by 800 CE, there was a well-established copper and gold trade.

Ethnicities changed, particularly in the north, as populations waxed and waned against each other, and territories shifted.

This period also saw a decline in Greenland megafauna, as a result of increasing population density in the interior, and more sophisticated hunting techniques. The population and range of megafauna, particularly camel and mammoth declined, and they were split into isolated populations. This decline was made up for by an increase in caribou populations. Megafauna also declined in the south and central basin sea mammal populations.

Rise of a Prot-Civilization

The slow percolation of elements of the Dorset cultural toolkit to the Saqqaq tribes of the South Basin had far-reaching effects.

The spread and use of the toggle harpoon changed the subsistence economy. Initially, it made hunting of sea mammals more effective. The rate of successful kills balanced against effort increased substantially.

The introduction of the kayak also changed hunting. The Dorset lands were far removed, so the diffusion of the Kayak accumulated a number of variations. No one quite built exactly the Dorset way, so there were improvisations and adaptations, workarounds. Often these failed, but the successful ones translated into innovations.

In the south basin, this evolved into a period of experimentation with forms, and the Dorset kayak diverged into umiaks, catamarans, outriggers and other skin boat variations, even wooden or partially wooden boats and rafts.

These boats and rafts allowed hunting expeditions to travel substantial distances along coastlines, or to venture increasing distances offshore.

At the very least, I think that they're going to take skin and bone, or skin and wood boats as far as they can possibly be taken. Some innovations, such as sails or nets might be a bit too big a jump. But they wouldn't be vital.

The thing with an inland sea like the Caspian, Mediterranean, the Red, the Black, the Persian Gulf, is that these are pretty placid places to take a boat around. Open ocean waters are scary and dangerous places, even under normal circumstances, and hellish in a storm. Sheltered interior seas on the other hand, involve calmer waters, safe harbors and land not too far away.

The Central Sea will provide a safe opportunity for a sedentary fishing culture to build very ambitious boats, and to go out into the water and even travel long distances. The Central Sea is stable; its currents regular, the changes from season to season are predictable.

With the ability to travel on a relatively safe and predictable sea, the southern Saqqaq can explore far beyond their normal ranges, they can explore most of the coastlines and river systems, meeting the natives and exchanging with them.

For instance, this allows for hunting ranges to expand. You're no longer limited by how far you can walk and how much you can carry. Travelling by boat, paddling or taking known currents, you can go much further, and carry much more out and back. You can dramatically expand your hunting territory. The south basin region was already the most densely populated area in Greenland, and the expansion of hunting territories and increased hunting efficiency, supported a steadily increasing population density.

In turn, this put increased pressure on the populations of sea mammals which formed the bulk of the subsistence economy. In the past, hunting pressure had resulted in local depletion and communities had been forced to disperse or relocate after a few years, or a generation or two. Because depletions tended to be local, once hunting populations dispersed or relocated, the recovery was usually quick.

The cumulative effects of new hunting innovation and increasing population, however, accelerated the problem. Larger and larger areas of the south basin began to see marine mammal population collapses, with recovery periods much slower.

The immediate effect was warfare and raiding along the South Basin, as different tribes competed violently for increasingly impoverished sea-hunting grounds. Accompanying this was increasing territoriality and formal territoriality centering around secondary food resources, such as fish runs, spawning grounds. Over time, treaties and arrangements between tribes attempted to allocate access to sea mammals, and preserve populations for sustainable harvest.

But neither warfare nor treaties could resolve the decline of sea mammals, the populations were heavily impacted and slow to recover.

The diets of the south basin Saqqaq shifted over time from 80% sea mammal protein - walrus, seal and beluga, to 80% fish catch. It's worth noting that the Central Sea is almost certainly a hyper-productive fishery, and this offers the potential for a proto civilization.

There is precedent - it appears that the Chimu culture in Peru became a settled stable culture relying on the fishery, and only later branched into agriculture. On the British Columbia coasts, the fishery allowed the Haida and other coastal communities to live in permanent villages and towns, to build

monumental totem poles, large houses, and develop a
prominent artistic tradition. Rich sea fisheries may be key in
other early civilizations, particularly around Lebanon or at the
mouth of the Persian Gulf.

Sea mammals aren't a terribly efficient diet. Basically, sea
mammals like seals and beluga consume thousands and
thousands of pounds of fish. So, if you switch from sea
mammals to fish, cut out the middlemen, you can actually
feed a lot more people ... assuming you've the technology to
catch them.

The early Saqqaq's technology was appropriate for spearing
seals and walrus, not good at catching large numbers. But
cultural exchange and shifts of lifestyle has allowed the
Saqqaq of the southern basin to acquire new tools and
innovations. This dietary shift had profound cultural impacts.
Fish harvest was a far more sustainable form of sustenance.
In particular, the decline of many fish-eating sea mammals
increased the available human harvest.

But key fishing grounds, river mouths, spawning runs, tended
to be geographically fixed. Sea mammals moved but
harvesting grounds didn't. This tended to result in
increasingly fixed communities.

The effort and process involved in fish harvest was
significantly different from sea mammal harvest. Taking a
walrus or a seal was an individual effort, or at the very least
the work of small hunting parties out in the field. A fish
harvest was a communal effort; harvests during a spawning
run procured thousands of pounds of fish, but often within
the span of a week or so. These fish had to be caught,
dressed, smoked or dried, and stored. This called for
systematic organization of community labor and divisions of
communal labor.

The transition from semi-permanent small communities of sea mammal harvesters, to larger permanent communities of fish harvesters was neither easy, rapid nor straightforward. It went back and forth. Efforts were abandoned or failed. Social organizations evolved, communities fought internally and externally, negotiated, experimented.

But over the course of several hundred years, the south basin came to be dominated by relatively sedentary, long term communities, exhibiting increasing social complexity, and extensive relationships with their neighbors. You'd see hierarchies, divisions of labor and specializations, complex alliances and relationships between settled communities. So something resembling a proto-civilization, or the beginnings of one, without agriculture. Overall, relatively sophisticated non-nomadic or transient indigenous people.

A Copper Trading Network

Typically, in subsistence societies, trade is like a game of telephone. Goods are passed hand through hand until they get to where they're consumed, or used, or stop being passed along. Now what this means is that 'stuff' can travel a long, long, long way. Meso-American obsidian all the way up to the Arctic Circle, Great Lakes copper down the Mississippi, tobacco as far as Hudson Bay. There are downsides to this. It's pretty damned slow. And it can be hit and miss.

And it's low volume - small amounts travelling, and heavily, heavily weighted to ritual and ceremonial objects, and small portable tools and items. Nobody wants to pass bulk and freight along hand to hand.

In any case, in most subsistence societies, the community usually has all of its key resources in or near its nomadic range, so they don't actually need a lot of outside stuff. And being a nomadic community, you don't want to have to schlep lots of stuff back and forth. You'd be surprised by how much weight is unnecessary, if you have to carry or drag it each day.

This is most of the Greenland historical trade networks. It's how the Saqqaq, Independence and Dorset cultures traded within themselves and between each other. For instance, it's how the Coastal Saqqaq are doing things around the Atlantic coasts. The Kayaks have enabled them to move a little further, a little faster, but there you go.

Boats are a potential game changer, in that, they offer an opportunity to travel further and carry more. But, at least initially, they aren't revolutionary - not when the model is small volumes and hand to hand.

Two things change trade dramatically.

One is population density. When population densities are small, people are spread thin, then there's not that much demand in any particular locale, and that 'telephone' trade system works pretty well. Population density though tends to create more demand than such diffuse networks can handle easily. As we can see, the south basin Saqqaq are building up rapidly.

The other is a particularly valuable trade good, one whose value is so extravagant that it overwhelms the sleepy telephone trade network and begins to drive a systematic trading system.

Which brings us to metals. The Saqqaq and their neighbors are Neolithic cultures, no question about that.

An import item for the south basin communities would be telluric iron from Disko Bay. Telluric iron existed naturally in relatively pure nodules. It could be harvested, and eventually beaten or ground into edges for cutting or chipping tools, and in fact, the local Inuit used it for these purposes. The Disko Bay iron was not the only metal finding its way into the trade network and into the south basin.

There's a second source of iron. Cape York is the site of an immense iron meteor, at least sixty or seventy tons, which fell a few thousand years ago. The meteorite fragmented, with eight large chunks composing 58 tons. Once again, in our history, the local Inuit made use of pieces of meteoric iron.

In this different history, it's almost certain that both Cape York and Disko Bay iron, in small but steady quantities, would have entered into the trade networks. Metals, iron, copper or bronze are always extremely valuable. It's certain that it would have shown up in increasing quantities in the south basin, and that the growing population would create a growing demand.

There's also a copper trade. Copper is a reasonable supposition. We can't count on it per se, since we don't know what copper deposits are under the ice, but it's pretty likely. Copper tends to clump, and in copper-rich areas, it can often be found in stream beds in the form of nuggets.

In both Alaska, and near the McKenzie Delta in Canada's Nunavut territory, the Dorset and the Inuit both learned to work copper and used it for tools. In the Great Lakes area, the Huron copper complex dug up raw copper and traded artifacts across North America. Copper use is the gateway to metallurgy for most civilizations.

Now the thing with copper is that the melting point is fairly low. It's not so low that you can melt it in a campfire or in your oven. You need more heat than that. But copper is fairly soft and malleable as metals go, and with the heat of a campfire you can warm it up so that it gets even more malleable. Easy to pound nuggets together, easy to pound an edge to it, or to shape it into something useful - an axe head, a knife, a scraper, a chisel - or something ornamental, ceremonial or religious trinkets, or jewelry like armlets, bracelets, rings and necklaces.

Given the geography of Greenland, it is certain that there would be accessible copper deposits in some of the river systems feeding into the Central Sea. It's equally certain that locals would have eventually made use of them, and that it would enter into trade networks.

And of course, copper is the gateway metal - so if you start messing around with that, you start messing around with similar metals that show up in nuggets and are soft enough to pound and heat into things - gold, tin, maybe silver or lead, iron if you're lucky. You get better and better at heating things up. Copper and tin mix together to form Bronze. Get hot enough temperatures, you don't have to mess with nuggets, you can melt the metal ore out of sand or rock. Enough heat and carbon, iron gets to steel. The Saqqaq just haven't been around and in place long enough to get to smelting or bronze. They'll stay as copper workers, or telluric iron workers, heating, pounding, annealing, yes. No alloys, no smelting.

But copper! Hey, that's desirable stuff. The Saqqaq have a close trade route to telluric iron in Disko Bay. Iron is terrific, don't get me wrong. Take an edge like you wouldn't believe, keeps an edge, sharpens, hardest stuff around. But man, it's a bitch to work! You have to pound away at that stuff for weeks to get something useful, and it don't merge easy, heating it in the fire makes no difference.

On the other hand, copper is a lot easier to work with. Copper is like play doh, pound away for a few hours or a day, you get what you want, you can merge nuggets, it heats up good; what's not to love. So even with iron, there would be a huge demand for copper. As much as they can get.

So the likely copper sources are up in the north basin Eastlands. In the region of those flowing glacial rivers. If you're going to find placer mineral deposits in Greenland, that's my bet. And, as with the Copper Inuit of Alaska and the Yukon, and of the Great Lakes people, it's likely to be discovered and taken up by the locals, and eventually end up in the slow trade networks.

So, I am visualizing copper as a key element in this telephone-like trade network up and down the Eastern Lands to the south basin. But once you introduce the boat, or the concept and techniques of the boats to the people of the south basin, then they go out into the water, farther and further. Increasing population creates more and more demand. The system of telephone trade wasn't delivering enough ... wouldn't that be an incentive to sailing up the Central Sea? It wouldn't necessarily be that long a sea trip, maybe 100 miles distance, maybe 500 or 600, depending on the point where copper deposits are closest to coastlines, and where the exploring community is.

The entire north/south length of the sea is only about 900 miles. So, with reasonable sophistication in boatbuilding - say a couple of hundred years practice and exploration - the voyage would be doable. Potentially, the sedentary communities, if they were motivated, could explore the entire coastlines of the Central Sea and its tributary rivers. The south basin Saqqaq could even set up temporary mining colonies at northern deposits, gathering copper for a few weeks or months each summer, the cooperative labor required for massive fish harvest, and the elements of sailing technology could allow for it.

So what we might have in the south basins, are communities that are sort of like a Proto-Carthage, or a Proto-Tyr, the source of fleets bravely venturing out into the vast north basin, creating trading posts, or founding seasonal mining colonies. You would probably see an exponential volume of copper coming into the lower basins.

If there's an intensive copper trade, you'll inevitably see other metals with similar qualities, gold, silver, tin and lead. Particularly gold - Gold also tends to form nuggets, and end up in river systems, just like copper. Because of its luster and its soft malleability, it often becomes sought out.

Once you have a high volume trading system, copper expeditions travelling the length of the basin, then you'll see other commodities also entering the bulk system: Mammoth and Walrus ivory for sure, amber perhaps, obsidian, exotic shells, musk ox hide, perhaps gemstones, soapstone and sandstone. These goods would concentrate in the southern basin, but small quantities would disperse throughout Saqqaq cultures, even out to the folk along the outer coasts.

This seems like a recipe for a dynamic and vibrant people, a pulsing proto-civilization, about to blossom and burgeon onto the world stage. It's ... romantic, it's ... beautiful.

Explosion of Art and Architecture

We begin to assemble the elements of our Proto-Civilization. A lifestyle shift to organized cooperative fisheries, rather than bands of sea mammal hunters. We see sedentary stable communities occupying territory and resources. Increased population. New technologies, particularly boats, and a centralized bulk trading network.

Population, free time, and overall wealth in the south basin gave rise to both craftsmanship and productivity and to demand. South basin communities sent out expeditions to harvest soapstone, sandstone, amber, ivory, chert and obsidian. But as often, they learned to trade, driving and systematizing existing local trading relationships into coherent trade networks that extended from the desert north to the southern coasts.

Iron and copper, however, were particularly important to the south basin for stonework and woodwork. Both the Inuit of the north and the Haida of the British Colombia coast had remarkable artistic traditions. But ironically, it took European contact to allow these traditions to flourish fully. Why? Because before European contact, they were limited largely to stone tools. Europeans brought metal tools which allowed them to engage in stonework or woodwork to a greater extent than had ever been possible before.

But the Saqqaq already have access to iron and copper, albeit in tiny quantities compared to Europeans. But it's there, and available.

A major outlet of the availability of metal tools and the increased skill in stone working was a widespread tradition of artistic stone carving. All arctic cultures, including the Saqqaq, the Dorset and the Inuit engaged in stone carving for ceremonial and ritual purposes. These usually involved smaller softer stones, like pieces of soapstone.

Copper and iron allow the south basin Saqqaq to be more ambitious and begin to reshape harder rock in the form of boulders. At first, boulders were simply used as parts of petroglyphs or megalithic erections - sometimes moved or turned, sometimes left where they were. Boulders were often etched or drawn with figures. With some boulders, the contours of the rock suggested faces or body shapes, and rock drawing emphasized these features. At some point, stone working techniques were used to enhance these natural shapes, with faces and figures carved into the stone.

Over time, this evolved steadily into carving boulders into humanoid or animal shapes, usually crouching or curled up, based on the original shape of the rock. Boulder carving became increasingly ambitious, with communities and artists reshaping increasingly large boulders and even cliff faces. Twenty and thirty foot sculpted rocks became almost common, with far larger efforts begun and sometimes concluded.

The artistic tradition included animals, including marine mammals, and humans, including males and females, dressed and undressed. Later archeologists would identify different artistic periods in these different subjects, but the reality was that the different subjects simply reflected different ceremonial or magical purposes, or different communities, or different constituencies within a community.

South basin cultures had sufficient surplus population and time that they could invest in stonework. Initially, this took the form of elaborate petroglyphs, boundary markers, fish traps, and practical structures. The availability of iron and copper for tools, however, meant that stone working leaped ahead, with a greater ability to carve, fracture and split, and dress stonework.

The Haida of British Colombia lived in an environment of tall trees, so that was their medium, and they created vast lodge houses and totem poles. This is the universal, you work with what you got - the Egyptians had stone and quarries, they built pyramids. The Mesopotamians lived on a flood plain, and so they baked bricks for their Ziggurats.

A post-glacial environment, Greenland was littered with stones and boulders. Naked rock had been crushed and broken many times by glaciers and earthquakes. As a result, throughout Greenland, even as far north as the polar desert, stone was a frequent building material, for walls, for fish traps, forming foundations for bone and hide structures. In the southern region, wood was more readily available, but also in demand for a number of purposes, including fuel.

Dorset igloo techniques, reaching the south basin, became the foundation for an architectural tradition of stonework. The same construction concepts that produced domed igloos lead the south basin peoples to create stone igloos, and to work dressed stone to create a variety of arched buildings and structures. South basin permanent fishing villages exhibited increasing architectural complexity and innovation, albeit sometimes on a trial and error basis, sometimes built up over a period of centuries, by the time of Norse contact.

The Limits of Proto-Civilization

When following this pathway into New Greenland, it's tempting to keep layering stuff on. This Proto-Civilization of Proto-City States around the south basin, these Neolithic, arctic analogues of ancient Greeks and Phoenicians ... how far could they get, what more could they achieve?

But there are limits, time is against them. The Proto-Civilization begins to emerge probably around 400 or 500 CE, and takes a couple of hundred years to mature, say 600 or 700 CE. But the Norse will be showing up in only a few hundred years. That's not much time left to accomplish big things.

Take boats - they've inherited and adapted fairly sophisticated skin boats from the Dorset, innovated, perhaps experimented with wooden boats and rafts, they've learned the stable currents and seasons of their placid sea. But boats have been developed independently by hundreds of cultures; they go back as far as 40,000 years.

Sails? That's been independently invented perhaps three or four times in history, they probably won't invent it, they don't really need it.

They won't invent literacy - again, that's only a handful of inventions, and really, only once in North America. Although they use copper and iron, they won't really invent smithing or smelting.

Agriculture is probably a step too far. They probably harvest wild plants regularly, may engage in some management practices. But it's not clear that there's any plant worth domesticating, or time to be able to do it.

Animal domestication? There's no domesticating fish or sea mammals. The caribou's cousin, the reindeer was domesticated or semi-domesticated by the Lapps, and there's some theory that musk ox were domesticated at one time. Maybe those might be domesticated here, maybe there's an option to domesticate salt tolerant camels, or moose, or tapirs. But domestication events are rare in history and unlikely here. As entertaining as it might be, I don't think that there's much chance of Mammoth riding Saqqaq warriors.

Astronomy? I think that they'll have a strong grasp on the seasons, and maybe calendars. But they'll probably be more interested in the northern lights as a source of augury, than the movements of stars.

In the end, there's a limit to what the time available grants, or the environment and resources allow.

The Norse Invasions, Erik the Red

Possibly around 976, possibly earlier, Gunnbjorn Ulfsonn is blown off course on a voyage from Norway to Iceland. He sights Islands or possibly land, but does not land there.

Instead, he makes his way back to Iceland. The story gets around.

Approximately 982, Erik the Red is exiled from Iceland for three years, for the crime of murder. Eric is an interesting guy; he was born around 950 or 960. Probably closer to 950 than 960, since his son Leif was born 971, and I can't imagine Erik fathering children at the age of 10. So, he was probably between 25 or thirty in 981. So, a relatively young man. A man in the prime of his life. A man with a wife, and presumably a network or relatives and kin.

Erik came from a violent background. He and his father were exiled from Norway when he was ten, for his father killing a man. They moved to Iceland, settling in a neighborhood called Dranga. This was 100 years into Iceland's colonization, and most of the good land has already been taken up. He was likely either a pretty marginal farmer, or a tenant. Following his father's death, Eric married into a wealthy family and inherited a large farm, and established a manor.

980-982 CE, Erik is doing well enough to have servants. Some of these servants accidentally caused a landslide that destroy a neighbor's house. The neighbor kills the servants, and Erik kills the neighbor.

That tells us a few things - Erik is relatively wealthy and powerful, a householder, with people under him. And he's violent, and people are pretty touchy. The whole incident seems to have left a cloud, and despite relative wealth and status, he's not welcome in the neighborhood after that.

He moves to a settlement on the islands of Oxney and Sudrey. Again, things go bad, fighting breaks out, and several people, including the two sons of Erik's neighbor, are killed. Erik went on trial, was found guilty of murder or manslaughter. He gets declared an outlaw and banished for three years.

Counting his dad, this is three incidents of murderous violence in a twenty year period, each incident escalating bigger and badder. Two other things come out of this - one is that Erik is not well liked by his neighbors. He's apparently some kind of interloper, and it's likely that he is pushing them. I wouldn't put it past him to be encroaching on fields, quietly stealing cattle, asserting his water rights, abrasively and aggressively.

Iceland is a settled place, and the only way you're going to really build yourself up there is if you push. But anywhere you push, it's going to get your neighbors' noses out of joint. And Erik doesn't seem to mind that, up to and including violence. He's very aggressive, very much a jerk.

But the other thing is, he's got a following. In Dranga, he's got a manor and servants. On Oxney and Sudrey, he's got enough supporters or followers that he seems to get the better of a full-fledged riot or local war against the entrenched locals. And of course, when he's exiled, he's not alone. He's got a ship full of followers, perhaps two or three. This also seems like a guy who lacked security in his early life, and who has consistently sought wealth and power, dominion over others and leadership, to make up for that lack. He seems driven. Overall, this is a guy who seems like he's going to be bad news for anyone he meets.

Getting back to 982, he's exiled for three years for murder or manslaughter. He's heard Ulfsonn's story from 976, so he decides to sail west. He ends up finding Greenland. He travels up and down the coast for a while, exploring. In our history, Greenland is uninhabited. Everywhere that Erik the Red goes is vacant land, waiting to be claimed. But it is also otherwise without apparent value.

Eventually, he returns home, claims he's found a terrific place that he calls Greenland, to encourage people to settle there.

25 ships went out, 14 made it to form a settlement. Eric eventually founds two, maybe three settlements in Greenland, he's elected leader.

But it's a pretty tough life. There's no one there to lord it over, it's raw virgin territory, and pretty miserable territory at that. The only way anyone gets anywhere is by working at it, so the whole place operates on individual one-man labor. There's little in the way of a convenient surplus to harvest, or to confiscate. It's tough to be a king there, because in the end, you have to break the fields and feed the damned goats, the same as everyone else.

In this timeline, Greenland is inhabited.

So what or who does Erik the Red meet? He won't encounter the Proto-Civilization developing around the south basin of the Central Sea. They're far inland, and as we've seen, it's really hard to get inland. At least, not early on.

Erik the Red sails west. Going by the currents, he could have gone northwest or southwest. I don't see him going north when he reaches Greenland. Along the East Coast, he's at some of the most inhospitable places around Greenland. The coast abuts the Eastern Mountain ranges, so you've got steep inhospitable rocky country, waterfalls and fast-moving rivers, small bergs calving. Fishing is good, but currents are treacherous. Further north are the sparse bands and tribes of the Independence Islanders and Peninsulares. But there's little motivation to go there.

He's likely to travel south, finding the relatively narrow lowland, but no rivers into the interior. He'll travel the coastal fjords, moving south. From about 65 latitude, it's about 700 miles, give or take, to the point where Eric the Red will later found the Eastern settlement of OTL, the first and largest of the three Norse settlements. We can assume that he explored at least that far in his initial voyages.

It's possible that he sailed up the western coast. He did have three years of exile time to kill. But it would be at least seven or eight hundred more miles sailing north to where he would reach Disko Bay or the exit channel joining the south basin to the Atlantic. I don't think that Erik the Red would have gone that far, either in old or new Greenland. Either reality, there's no motivation for him to head north. He would have been most interested in the southern lands. North, up the west side, would not have been appealing. Old Greenland, he would have been most interested in potential settlement/landing areas, the best sites for an ambitious man to found a community. Of course, in Old Greenland, all he met were walrus and seal, the occasional caribou and a few stands of birch and scrub in the southern fjords.

This New Greenland though, is comparatively richer and more fertile. That's not necessarily obvious from the coastline and fjords. Most of the southern coast borders on highlands and hills, brutal terrain with steep elevations, partially glaciated mountain or hill tops, and highland arctic tundra. The coastlines are better (more fertile and biologically productive, more visiting caribou) than OTL, but not that much better. They give no indication of the interior landscape. And there's a distinct lack of rivers draining into the ocean that would give any kind of interior access.

So in this New Greenland, he's stuck with the coasts. He travels a few hundred miles along these coasts, maybe a thousand, continually moving south. Who does he find?

Saqqaq of the Outer coast Fords

These people will have been in the areas anywhere from a few hundred to a thousand years. The outer fjords were not settled quickly or easily. The land was better in the interior, and so most Saqqaq tended to go there. But over time, a few tribes ended up on the western coast for one reason or another, and they began to settle, leapfrogging from fjord to fjord, making their way to the southern tip of Greenland, and then slowly up the eastern coast.

They've done better than the historical Saqqaq, who never got this far south, spreading further south and east along the coasts. Partly, because this is a more gentle Greenland than the one we know, the landscape a little more productive, mountain camels, caribou and musk-ox a little more common, the seas a little more productive. Their tool kit is a little bit better. Through diffusion from the Dorset, they have crude kayaks, possibly toggle harpoons, possibly igloos.

They subsist principally on sea mammals, with their diets supplemented by fish, birds, the occasional caribou or hill-dwelling herbivore, and whatever edible vegetation they can scrounge. The Coastal Saqqaq are nomadic, but a rigorous type of nomad, moving seasonally along well-established routes. Their environment is Spartan, the harvesting and feeding grounds, the sea mammal haul outs, the fishing runs, the caribou pathways and even berry patches are very specific and do not change from year to year. Their lives are almost regimented - their year consists of moving from one location to another, always specific locations, for specific times.

Regimentation allows them to construct semi-permanent dwellings along their route, stone or hide and branches, with larders, skinning or drying racks. Their fjords are marked with dwellings and campsites, sometimes occupied intermittently over hundreds of years. Their environments are marginal, and the Saqqaq colonization of this south was slow. The kayak has made fishing and seal hunting easier in the summer, and it's also allowed bands to communicate and contact each other more easily, and to travel a little more easily.

This communication allows for occasional trade, mostly in ceremonial objects, medicines, small trinkets and handicrafts. We don't see the centralized bulk commodity trade network operated by the south basin Saqqaq. Rather, on the coast, it's old style, the trade routes are hand to hand, an extremely slow game of telephone, with low volumes.

It's mostly local trade, the bulk of it depending on whether a tribe's available resources include something like a particularly vital deposit of obsidian or flint, or useful soapstone or pipestone, or a desirable amber or shellfish. A desirable item, like a bit of pipestone for a ceremonial pipe might be mentioned in one gathering, and eventually show up years later.

Once in a while, some artifact or ceremonial object from the interior, a copper tool or a gold amulet might show up.

The Coastal Saqqaq are aware of the idea of strangers, albeit these are mostly the bands or tribes in the adjacent fjords, and tales of the bands or tribes further up and down the coast. Like everything else in Coastal Saqqaq lives, their visits to and from these strangers are heavily regimented, taking place at specific times and places, and accompanied by appropriate ceremonies and arrangements. But they at least have the idea of strangers and trade.

The Coastal Saqqaq have never seen a ship or ships like those of Erik the Red. They have at least the idea of boats from their kayaks. But Erik's knars are immense, capable of carrying an entire tribe, men, women, and children. They know oars from their paddles but have never imagined sails. Theirs is a culture where trees are sparse, and wood is valued. The sheer volume of wood in use, and skillfully put together is mind blowing.

The wealth represented in the Norse tools and possessions is astonishing. The Norse themselves are utterly alien - the strangers who live in fjords up and down the coast speak the language obviously, but no meaning can be gleaned from these new strangers. Erik's arrival will be miraculous.

The Norse Invasions, First Contact

Erik's first contact may be with these people directly, which would be a mutual shock. Or he may well have encountered their works first - empty and unoccupied dwellings and sheds, the remains of cooking sites, skinning or tanning rocks, while they are off somewhere else in their subsistence cycle. If unoccupied, he's likely to find several similar places in succession, the ghostly remnants of unseen people - the Saqqaq elsewhere in their cycle. It will depend on when he arrives, where they are in their cycle.

But whether immediately or not, Erik the Red and his fellows will eventually encounter the Saqqaq. He and his Norse will find them a timid but curious people. Few in numbers, scrawny and impoverished, marginal savages leading a thin existence. Perhaps easily bullied, easily stormed and run off. The Coastal Saqqaq are decent hunters, even ambitious, but not warlike. The women are available for the taking, there may be a tradition of sharing.

Initial contact might be relatively peaceful. After all, Erik has only a few ships and a handful of men, maybe no women, likely no cattle. He and his men are probably careful and hungry and cautious.

But Erik, from the little we know of him, is an impulsive man, quick to anger, short on patience, ambitious and overbearing, not prone to moral reflection.

There are language barriers. Cultural barriers. And while the Saqqaq grasp the idea of peaceful meetings with strangers and even trade, their approaches are very regimented and formal, and Erik and his crew will not be familiar with them. In particular, their trade is often a slow thing, a relationship of exchanges year after year after year ... while Erik is a 'right now' kind of guy.

So, odds are, things are likely to go bad, sooner or later. Eric, after all, is a violent man, and he comes from a culture which has been raiding and despoiling Europe for centuries.

The people he encounters will be smaller, weaker, unused to violence, and ill prepared. They'll lack steel or iron weapons, or any kind of martial tradition. Initial encounters might be peaceful, but the minute Erik figures out he can get away with killing these people ... the clock starts ticking.

Erik will sail the coast, making first contact again and again. Each contact a brand new and utterly disastrous experience for the Coastal Saqqaq he encounters. While there is communication back and forth along the coast, it is a slow and regimented thing with its own pace. Erik will almost certainly outrun it. Each group of Saqqaq will have no idea he is coming, and thus no way to defend themselves.

Eric slaughters his way up down the coast, raiding and looting what little there is to be looted, despoiling food caches and guaranteeing ruin in his wake. He finds some good locations to overwinter, likely the future sites of Eastern and Western settlements. Clears out the locals, perhaps taking some women, enslaving some men, and builds a little community, a safe haven and fortress from which he can raid.

Over time, he learns enough language, or the slaves learn enough Norse for communication. He shifts from slaughtering communities to forcing tribute, whatever they can offer - food, hides, ivory, trinkets. He may even inquire as to the source of the occasional gold or copper item and hear garbled tales of cities in the interior.

When his exile finally ends, he abandons the slaves, or slaughters them, or takes them back ... and returns home with a cargo of valuable ivory and trinkets, and tales of a green and fertile land, with nothing holding it but a few handfuls of wretches easily conquered.

The Norse Invasion, Erik Returns

In Old Greenland history, Erik the Red came back to Iceland, talked the place up spectacularly, calling it Greenland in one of history's most flagrant cases of false advertising. In 985, he persuaded twenty-five ships to come back to Greenland with him to found a colony.

Fourteen of those ships made it. Erick settled at a location called Brattahhlio, in Tunariliq fjord on the southern tip of Greenland. This area is sheltered from the Atlantic and contains some of the best agricultural land in Greenland. Presumably, Eric found it and decided on it during his first voyage.

How are things different in this alternate? Erik comes back, substantially richer, with a cargo of trinkets, ivory, furs and hides, perhaps slaves, maybe even a little gold. There's probably a lot more interest. Erik's tales are likely more extravagant, and this time he's got actual proof. If any of his men are talkative, they'll have better things to say.

So, is it still just 25 ships? Or more. We don't know enough of the politics to really decide. Maybe 25 ships were Erik's entire clan group, and that's the maximum. Maybe a few more ships would have come along.

It's likely that Erik, with visions of wealth dancing before his eyes, would have wanted to claim the whole place for himself, by hook or crook. He might have exaggerated the ferocity of the natives. Or claim trade deals were exclusively with him. He had the advantage in knowing the route and knowing the coast.

So, assume 25 ships, no more than 50, and about 14 or 20 making it. Assume that Erik sets up his base of operations in the same location.

What happens next?

Things don't go exactly the way they did in our history, that fjord is too nice a spot to go unoccupied. If it's his old site, he's probably killed off the natives and slaves. But he likely selects at least a few new sites as well, unfortunately for the people living there. So, the Coastal Saqqaq are killed, enslaved, or driven off. Likely, a combination of the three. There might be initial coexistence, but the lifestyles are too distinct and too incompatible. Even basic concepts of property are different. Relations will go south, even in the best circumstances.

Erik, in this timeline, is much more likely to go up and down the coast doing some trading, raiding or tribute collecting. Probably not much in the first couple of years. Farming and getting established, collecting and training slaves, building a fort, sorting out the local Skraelings. But local trade is going to happen. Possibly, if Erik behaves badly enough, the Saqqaq up and down the coast may gather and mass for an attack. Not likely to turn out well for the Saqqaq. The Norse are used to fighting, and it's not like they can just flee back home.

But assuming local trade, and a decently valuable cargo back to Iceland, this may inspire settlers to come at a greater rate.

In Old Greenland, the three settlements never made it past 10,000, and probably hit fewer than 2500 people max. This is an interesting contrast to Iceland, which seems to have filled up within sixty years of discovery, going from zero to 40,000 people.

Would we see comparable expansion in Greenland? Probably not. Greenland's settlement is probably drawing mainly from Iceland. So, the base population, while growing rapidly, is still pretty small. You'll get some contributions from Norway, but these are Norwegians who in our history would have settled Iceland first and stayed.

Greenland also has a native population - Iceland was uninhabited. The Norse didn't mind settling or trying to displace locals - they did it to Ireland, to England, in France, so that's not a huge obstacle. But going to an uninhabited place where you didn't have to deal with locals was probably a big draw in the first place, and that makes leaving to deal with local schlubs less attractive.

With more value, and more potential land, Erik has a lot less ability to maintain a monopoly. It's likely that in the next twenty or thirty years, there's significantly more settlers, including settlers with less or no allegiance to Erik. This may imply less cohesion and perhaps genuine conflicts between the Norse groups. Erik was known for his temper, and I don't think he'd appreciate interlopers pissing in his swimming pool. It may even come to violence. There may be an effort to drive people away.

Equally, more groups definitely equals more conflicts with the Coastal Saqqaq. So, off the top of my head, I'll estimate maybe 2500 to 5000 settlers in the first 30 years. Maximum 10,000 to 15,000 at the end of the first sixty years, strung out in a handful of settlements along the southern coast, like a string of pearls, evicting the Saqqaq from choice fjords, enslaving and slaughtering numbers of them.

The other significant issue is exploration. We don't have a good read on Norse explorations of Old Greenland. We know that they made it as far north on the Eastern side as Disko Bay, which became a popular walrus hunting ground. We also know that they made it to Baffin Island, which they called Helluland (The term translates as: Rock Land - Truth in Advertising!). Around 1000 AD, Leif Erikson got blown off course found Vinland, discovering North America.

So let's assume that the principal coastal explorations of New Greenland, at least up to the point where it's not completely horrible — say, latitudes 70 or 74, take place in the first forty years, 890 to 930. Most of this exploration is going to focus heavily on the Southern coasts. The exterior just gets less and less interesting and desirable the further north you go, and the best coastal places to settle are all in the far south.

The Thule Arrive from the North

The Thule people were the ancestors of the modern Inuit. Approximately 3000 years ago, they had crossed over from Siberia, settling in Alaska. There for almost 2000 years, they had resided quietly, not causing too much trouble.

Then around 1100 CE, they'd exploded out of their northern refuge, west into the Bering Peninsula, throughout Alaska, and East driving across the Canadian Arctic to Hudson's Bay. They'd gone expanded north throughout the Canadian archipelago, and crossed the Bay into the Labrador Peninsula. By about 1200 or 1300 CE, they'd crossed into Greenland. Without warning, they'd overtaken a vast stretch of territory, driving the Dorset into extinction.

The best guess seems to be that the Medieval Warm Period had destabilized the Dorset's delicate balance with nature, allowing the Thule to overrun them. The other factor was that the Thule had perfected a more advanced Arctic tool kit, adding bows and arrows, dog sleds and umiaks (large skin boats capable of carrying a dozen or more people). The dog sleds and umiaks enabled the Thule to travel further and faster, to range more widely and carry far more resources with them than the Dorset.

But as disastrous as the Thule were for the Dorset, and as masterful as their arctic kit was, there was a limit to their ability. To the south, they were unable to displace the Dene, the Cree or the Innu, who resolutely defended their territories.

In our history, of course, the Thule occupied the whole of Greenland eventually, arriving south by about 1400 or 1500, replacing the departing Norse. The Dorset were probably already extinct in Greenland by the time the Thule arrived, or perhaps were driven out in Greenland, as they were everywhere else.

But in this history, things turn out a little differently.

In this new history, as in the old, the Thule enter northern Greenland. There they find the Dorset and the process of displacement begins. Elsewhere it was simple enough, the Thule with their dogsleds and umiaks are far more mobile, and mobile in greater numbers with more tools and resources, and displace the Dorset. That is how it goes here, somewhat.

But the mixture of folk across the northern half of Greenland is different. The Independence cultures, including their Island cultures, have been forced into marginal niches, but have become very sophisticated at holding these niches. They're experts at utilizing barren lands, and the Thule make little headway. In large areas, the Thule successfully push out the Dorset out of much of the north. The result is waves of population displacement as the Dorset move south. In turn, the Dorset intrude on Saqqaq lands further south creating disruption. Nevertheless, the Dorset manage to hold on in certain areas. The northern quarter becomes a polyglot of cultures and languages.

The Thule reach the Central Sea. Their Umiaks allow them to sail along and dominate the northern parts of the sea. But by this time, the Proto-Civilization of the South Basin Saqqaq are ranging widely with their own improvised boats. The umiak are superior craft, faster more agile. The Thule become pirates of the northern sea, battling for dominance with the southern people.

Elsewhere, the Dorset are more difficult to displace. Firmly established along the Atlantic Western Coast, the Dorset and Saqqaq communities have through competition tempered each other, ably and efficiently defending their territories. There the Umiaks give no advantage.

Instead, the Thule move into the thinly populated western table lands where their dog sleds give them unparalleled mobility. Unable to practice their sea based subsistence, they begin to follow the caribou herds migrating back and forth.

Already familiar with dogs as draft animals, some of them begin to apply similar principles to the caribou. This never happened with the Thule or Inuit in our history. Their lives were always tied to the sea, and an annual subsistence cycle that precluded dependence on the herds. The Thule/Inuit hunted caribou when the herds came through in season, and in other seasons, they hunted seals. To have committed to caribou year round would have meant giving up seals and other parts of their subsistence economy.

But in northern Europe and Siberia, indigenous peoples like the Sammi and the Nenets did embrace a lifestyle centered around the reindeer herds, and did semi-domesticate, or domesticate the reindeer. The reindeer are genetically identical to caribou. So it's reasonable to assume that the Thule, forced into a new path, would adopt a similar trajectory and even semi-domesticate or domesticate the caribou.

Within a generation or two, they shift to become a caribou herding, big game hunting nation of nomadic Mongols, migrating back and forth almost the length of western Greenland, neighbors and allies to their cousins, the pirate nation of the Central Sea. Their mobility, weaponry and lifestyle make them akin to the later plains Indians, or the earlier Mongols. They achieve a reputation as unparalleled warriors, unrelentingly fierce.

Their relationships with their neighbors, the Independence tribes, the Dorset, the various tribes of Saqqaq are complex and often hostile. The Thule after all, are feared, fearsome and expansive. But they are also willing participants, sometimes aggressively so, in the extensive trade networks. Peaceable relations do occur.

With this comes cultural diffusion. Thule tools, weapons, artifacts and loan words find their way into the south. Thule trade goods, spread. The most significant Thule innovation are dog sleds and draft animals, adopted off and on along the coasts, embraced heartily by the South Basin Saqqaq and their proto civilization.

The Thule are latecomers to the party. By the time they arrive, the Norse will, in some fashion or other, be well established, or at least well known in the south. The peoples of the south basin, and of the southern reach will likely be strongly altered by the Norse experience.

But for the northern three fourths of Greenland, where Norse agriculture or herding can't even pretend to take hold, the Norse impact will be minimal. Most people's lives and traditions will not be different from their ancestors of centuries before. So the impact of the Thule may be immense in the north.

The Fall of Atlantis – Page 182

Ultimately, for both the Norse in the south, and the Thule in the north, it was the Medieval Warm period that triggered each of their explosive expansions, and caused each to sweep across vast sections of the world. It was the Medieval Warm period that saw the rise of the south basin proto-civilization.

As to what the Thule find in the south, centuries after Viking contact, we will withhold speculation. What we will say is that in the coming centuries, the Little Ice Age begins. In our history, it spelled doom for the Greenland Norse. In this history, the proto civilization and the Norse will struggle… and these Greenland Thule, who have evolved to so resemble the Mongols and the warlike plains Indians, they'll be forced south… That could be interesting, especially for whoever they find down there.

It is another element added to the intricate picture, already complicated by the Norse.

The Norse Invasions, Search for the Central Sea

The Norse steadily dominate the southern coastlines. But mostly only the southern coastlines. Past a certain latitude, the Saqqaq or Dorset hold their own – The climate unsuitable for Norse agriculture or herds, and the coastal territories useless, except for occasional slave raids or pirating sea mammals.

What about the Interior? That's tricky. There are practically no good access ways into the Interior. The coastlines are rocky and high and difficult to penetrate. There are places where you could travel overland into the Interior, in gaps between mountain ranges, but that's a lot of walking. There are almost no good river systems to sail up and find your way to the interior. And there may not be a lot of incentive.

The only real access to the interior is the outlet river/channel from the South Basin near Disko Bay and is probably identified sometime between 900 and 910. That may not be easily passable or navigable.

Depends on how ugly it is as to whether and how soon the Norse want to try going up it. They're sailors. They're not bringing along a lot of horses. So, they go up rivers in their boat, and then they have to physically drag that boat overland to get around rapids and portages. A lot depends on how far and how often the channel is navigable. If it's relatively smooth sailing, then I think we may see the Norse reach the interior South Basin as early as 920 to 930.

If it's a hellish succession of waterfalls, rapids and cataracts, with broken ugly terrain all around, they'll probably say 'heck with this' particularly when there are easier, richer pickings along the coast. Which may mean the interior gets put off a lot longer, say 960 to 990.

The Norse actually got up to some pretty strange places in our universe. They were able to sail around the European coast into what is now northern Russia, and sail down rivers and portages to reach the Caspian and Black Seas. That's how they got involved with the Byzantine Empire. It all depends on how difficult/brutal the passageway from the South basin to the Atlantic is. If it's just a series of waterfalls, cataracts and rapids, with rough country surrounding it, they might say the heck with it. Or if it's easy, they may sail a fleet of knars and go 'nice country, we'll take it.'

It's quite possible that Erik the Red may simply concentrate on his little kingdom and his string of settlements along the south coast of Greenland. He has the natives to enslave and terrorize, tribute to exact, taxes to collect. In comparative terms, New Greenland is much wealthier for him than Old Greenland could ever be. It could keep him busy.

It's not likely that the enslaved Coastal Saqqaq in the deep south have any clear idea of what lies in the interior - cannibals, savage tribes, monstrous beasts, evil spirits. Mostly the coastal peoples will be insular, knowing themselves, knowing their immediate neighbors and not much else.

Of course, there may be some motivation to try and get to the South Basin sooner rather than later. Remember that some of the key trading goods along the coast that aren't locally crafted are coming from the south basin - this may include worked telluric iron, copper, mammoth ivory and even gold.

Particularly gold. If Erik the Red finds a few bits of gold in his raids or his tributes, he's smart enough to know that natives didn't produce it. He'll want to find out where it came from, and eventually, he'll get stories or legends of mighty cities of gold in the interior - half local fancy, half the desperate things you'll say when someone is roasting bits of you in a fire. And if there's gold, then Erik, or his men, or his successors will want it - or to find its source.

And the South Basin peoples have strong trading connections to the Disko Bay and adjacent coastal communities. If the Norse are able to communicate at all with the coastal Saqqaq in that region, they'll know that there's something worth investigating further in. Raids or forced tribute will produce more gold, more iron, more ivory around this area, a sure sign that there's something deeper.

So let's say that between 915 to 964, the Norse finally encounter the closest thing Greenland has to a sophisticated, organized series of sedentary societies - the Proto-Civilization of the south basin. That gets interesting.

Norse and South, What Happens Next?

And here, we'll pause the history of New Greenland, at that pregnant moment when the Norse explorers pass among wondrous megalithic sculptures, to rise a hill and gaze silently down at what they hoped was a city of gold.

It won't be like anything they've ever seen or imagined. There will be roads and paths, but no farmers' fields and no herds, few stone and wooden outbuildings. Instead, there are domes and fluting arches everywhere, protective stone walls and fortifications surrounding it, opening on a harbor filled with boats and rafts but none with sails, and beyond that an immense sea stretching off to the horizon. It'll be smaller than they expected, perhaps a few hundred people. Visibly prosperous but not wealthy. What will they make of it? Will they do?

What happens next?

We will leave that to the reader, offering only a few thoughts.

By this time, the Norse will have mastered Saqqaq dialects, or their slaves will have mastered Norse. In practical terms, it will be the same thing. The Norse and the 'cities' of this proto-civilization will be able to speak together, if they wish.

If there is gold, then it's likely that the true gold fields are far up along the eastern shores of the Central Sea. The Norse will not find an Eldorado, though they may find enough to whet their appetite. The true glory is still far beyond and very hard to reach. But even without gold, there may be other wealth to claim - mammoth or walrus ivory, amber, other portables.

At the very least, there may be land and slaves, since the interior lands are probably friendlier to Norse agriculture than the miserable coastal fjords. They may not even have to fight for that land, since the south basin peoples do not practice agriculture yet - they're people of the sea. They'll probably

not object if the Norse start taking up interior plots of land
that are useless to them.

Through Europe, the Norse were feared for raiding and
looting. They might try that route here. But the south basin
peoples are not like the peaceful isolated tribes in the coastal
fjords. The people of this proto civilization understand war,
they wage it on each other, and on the nomadic barbarians of
the southern reaches. There aren't that many Norse and
they're a long way from home. It could well end very badly.

With the Aztec and the Inca, these were empires full of ill-
treated conquered peoples. The Conquistadores simply
offered the subject peoples a better deal, and they rose up and
went with the Spaniards. Here there is unlikely to be a
dominant empire with hordes of resentful tribes as subjects.
More likely, you'll see something resembling the Greek or
Phoenician City States, suspicious, squabbling, perpetually
bickering and at war, but perhaps willing to unite in the face
of a greater threat.

Or things might go in more complicated directions. Perhaps
the Norse simply trade, perhaps they'll set up trading stations,
somewhere between Disko Bay and the south basin,
someplace that offers good farmland. What the Norse can
offer would be incredibly valuable to the south basin Saqqaq,
woven cloth, nets, blacksmithed iron and steel items, and far
more and better iron than they've ever had before. I could see
the south basin peoples warring upon each other for the
Norse trade. Or the Norse become involved in south basin
politics, manipulating factions and communities. Or perhaps
the Norse conquer communities or the whole south basin,
setting themselves up as a temporary or permanent ruling
class, as they so often did in Europe.

Whatever happens, the south basin peoples will be
transformed by contact with the Norse. That is inevitable.

New kinds of boats and boat techniques, sails will be revolutionary, fishing nets, writing and literacy, agriculture, horses, cattle, sheep and goats, pagan and Christian gods, mining, smelting, blacksmithing and metalworking. The south basin will be awash with new tools, new products, new ideas and new techniques. Food production, from enhanced fishing, from new animals and agriculture will expand, populations will explode.

The hunger for what the Norse offer will be insatiable, and that will transform societies. Gold might have been valued in the south basin, but it was stable within the local economies. Now it's the key to purchasing from the Norse, they'll be crazy for the Norse trade, and all you need to get anything and everything from the Norse will be gold. The importance of gold will skyrocket, there'll be major expeditions north to collect it, wars over it, perhaps permanent or semi-permanent mines and fortifications far up in the north basin. Norse goods and Norse desires will transform them.

In the long run, the odds are against the Saqqaq. The explosive flowering of their proto civilization brought by Norse contact may result in collapse. No new world civilization survived European contact unscathed, most were wiped out. That may well be the ultimate result here.

The south basin proto civilization may not survive, between pandemics, conquest and settlement, they may, in the end, be swept away, reduced to second class citizens in their own communities, replaced by new Norse settlements. I think that would be rather sad.

The rest of the Saqqaq, the Dorset and the Independence cultures elsewhere in New Greenland will survive. Norse agriculture and animal husbandry will really only work well in the south. Beyond the south basin, and the river lands south of that, apart from a few mining and harvesting stations, there's little to attract the Norse. The lands will support only subsistence economies, and a handful of trading posts. The changes and transformations will not come from the Norse, but from the Thule.

History never stops, and it won't stop for this alternate Greenland. The next centuries will see waves of transformation, from the Norse, the Thule, the Little Ice Age and beyond. This Greenland's history will become part of the world's history.

But this is the moment we'll pause the history of New Greenland, when the Norse explorers rise a hill and gaze silently down at the Sammaq proto-civilization. And at that moment, anything can happen next…

Pandemics?

Elsewhere, in the coming centuries, contact between Europeans and Natives introduced new diseases which devastated native populations. In some places, die-offs reached 90%. New Greenland might escape that fate for a while - New Greenland isn't being settled directly from Europe, but from a small intermediate population in Iceland, the numbers aren't large. So, there may not be much disease transmission, at least not in the beginning.

Iceland itself seems to have avoided pandemics until about 1401, at which point it killed off half the population, and then a generation or two later, something hit again that wiped out half the population again. Given that it killed off half the Icelanders in 1401, and possibly meant the death knell of Old Greenland (lots of free land and better opportunities back in Iceland to emigrate to), it would likely be horrible for a naïve virgin soil population in New Greenland.

The problem with virgin soil epidemics is that since there's no resistance, everyone gets it at the same time. Which means that there's no one to keep fires going, so people freeze; no one to catch and prepare food, so people starve; no one to carry fresh clean water, so dehydration; no one to look after the sick, so they don't recover. The society, the tribe, the members that would have kept things running and allowed people to recover are all sick, so with no one to help, everyone dies.

For the south basin Saqqaq, a lot would depend on when the pandemics struck. If is hit during the summer, particularly during a food gathering season, then it's doubly devastating. People go down, not only are there no caregivers, but there's no food or water sources, no fuel, that's all in the process of being harvested, starvation and dehydration rolls up already weakened immune systems. People are moving, it spreads everywhere quickly.

Hit in the winter, people are sick around stockpiles of food, water and firewood. They still die in droves, but food and water is readily available, the victims have a chance to recover, weakened immune systems aren't overwhelmed, there's less travel and communication, the rate of transmission slows and more chance of burning itself out locally. But even in the best case, it hits them hard.

Extinctions?

After four centuries in Old Greenland, the Norse died off. Perhaps they went extinct there, perhaps the remnants simply gave up and went back to Iceland, or were taken by pirates, or wiped out by the Inuit. The stories differ.

But even before it vanished, the Greenland colony was in trouble. There were a number of factors in play. The little ice age was kicking in, and it was making farming more and more difficult. Barley could no longer be grown, the Norse were living on their herds and growing hay. Trees weren't growing, so they couldn't build or maintain boats for fishing.

They were dependent on trade with Iceland and Europe. But then Denmark changed the rules of trade, prohibiting trade between Greenland and Iceland, and requiring everything to go through them. That made things more expensive for Greenland, it cost them a lot more to import and export. And the value of their exports dropped - their most valuable export was Walrus Ivory, and that was being outcompeted by African Ivory.

It turns out though, that there's more to the story. It seems that researchers have done studies of the Walrus Ivory coming from Greenland, and guess what, as time went on, there was less and less of it, and what there was, was poorer and poorer quality, coming from smaller and younger walruses. What that shows, is that the Greenlanders weren't just being outcompeted by better African Ivory. They were steadily wiping out their Walrus populations, driving them into extinction. They had to keep travelling further and further from home to catch Walrus, and as they killed off the ones with the biggest tusks, they kept working their way down until they were wiping out juveniles who barely had tusks.

We've talked about this before - what spurs commercial trade. Density of population, demand, accessibility. Through the 17th and 18th centuries, rapacious European expeditions literally wiped out entire populations of sea otters, seals, whales and walrus through the north, driving them into extinction wherever they could reach them. The European populations were huge, the demand incredible, they just tore through, searching out populations of animals and literally eradicating them.

The Fall of Atlantis – Page 191

This doesn't speak well for the fate of New Greenland. There will be much greater populations of Walrus, and Mammoths, but the demand for ivory and hides may well be bottomless and insatiable. In the Central Sea, the Walrus will be easy prey. Walrus and Mammoths may well be extirpated, many animals may well be wiped out. Caribou may survive, their herds seem fairly resilient. Musk Ox may or may not.

It doesn't have to end badly. It seems a shame to explore a New Greenland, and simply bring it all to ruin. I like the idea of a New Greenland where walrus and whales cavort in the inner sea, where a Saqqaq nation Europeanizes but survives to contribute something unique to the world, where Woolly Mammoths roam the plains.

If we dream of a better, more interesting world, perhaps we should keep it that way.

The End

A Note and More Books by the Author

Thank you for taking the time out to read my little book. If you've skipped to the end, looking for an apology, well... Sorry? Also, no refunds.

If you did like these excursions, might I recommend other books in the series: *The Dawn of Cthulhu* and *The Bear Cavalry, the True (Not!) History of the Icelandic Bear*. In addition, I'll also recommend the two-part alternate history chronicle of World War II in South America – *Axis of Andes* and *New World War*.

What else do I have to offer? Well, I have trilogy of collections of horror stories, starting with *Giant Monsters Sing Sad Songs*, and a pair of funny fantasy collections imaginatively titled *Drunk Slutty Elf,* and a fantasy murder mystery, *The Mermaid's Tale*.

For non-fiction, I have three kick ass *Doctor Who Pirates Histories*, and *LEXX Unauthorized*, the chronicle of a cult sci fi series.

Leave a review. Mention it on your blog, or your Facebook. Say nice things. Toss me a couple of stars. Appreciation is a wonderful thing and it can get hard to get noticed. Reviews help.

denvaldron.com

Drunk Slutty Elf and Other Stories

Hilarious Science Fiction and Fantasy

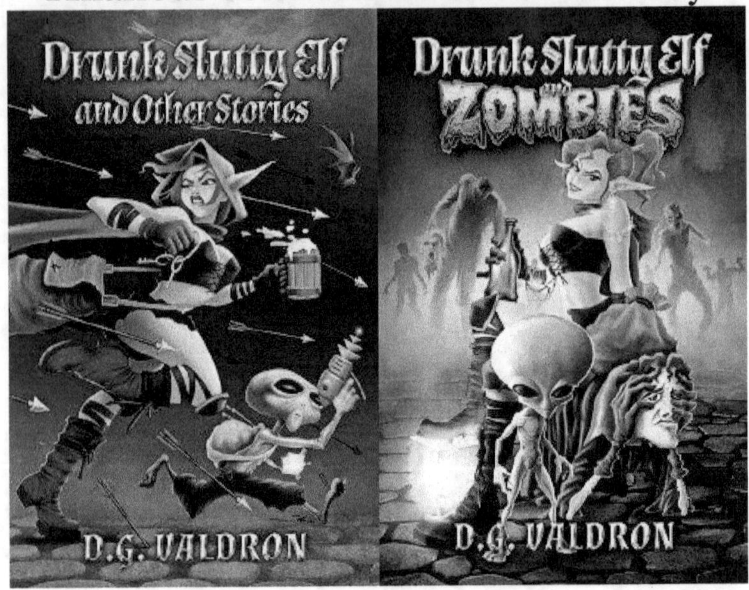

plus the sequel

DRUNK SLUTTY ELF

AND ZOMBIES!!!

Two volumes of savage, satirical, subversive wicked, funny, frantic science fiction and fantasy. Demented ghost hunters, frustrated aliens and many more.

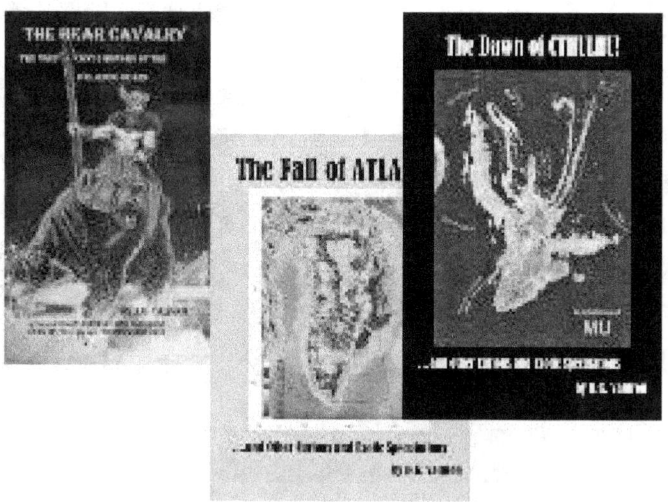

ALTERNATE REALITIES

A Trilogy or Strange New Worlds

The Dawn of Cthulhu - The Secret History of H.P. Lovecraft's Cthulhu Cult; Lost Continents Found – real and legendary; The Monsters of Sesame Street, is a light hearted examination of Muppets as if they were actual animals.

The Fall of Atlantis – Retroverse, An Accidental Cinematic Universe of 50's Sci Fi movies, Greenland Without the Ice, Rome Crosses the Atlantic, and the Rise and Fall of Atlantis, an ecological catastrophe.

The Bear Cavalry, the True (Not!) History of the Icelandic Bears, an off the wall, short novel about the Viking domestication of bears, their evolution into a medieval cavalry Bonus novelette, The Sharebear Apocalypse.

HEARTS IN DARKNESS

A Trilogy of Horror Collections

Giant Monsters Sing Sad Songs – The connection between the author of the Necronomicon and a boy in Providence; a girl who meets the last Sasquatch, a poet who shares abandoned Tokyo with a Kaiju…

What Devours Also Hungers – The unkillable killers in masks are recruited into the army, vampires and their hunters, serial killers, monsters and niore

There Are No Doors in Dark Places – A childlike cancer that talks to its owner; A single mother drawn into dark magic; A man who turns into a different monster each night, a pregnant woman finding her body being stolen from her; and many more.

AXIS OF ANDES

NEW WORLD WAR

A History of WWII in South America

Berlin, 1937, Adolph Hitler and his cabinet meet with a strange delegation from Ecuador. The delegates from the small South American nation beg for help, fearing an impending invasion from their rival, Peru. What happens at that meeting sets in motion a chain of events that lights the entire continent on fire. Nations are in ruins, and the map of Latin America will be changed beyond recognition.

The Pirate Histories!

 What's a Pirate's History, you ask? They're things that they don't want you to know about, or that they don't care about, things that are great and marvellous and intriguing... but unapproved. It's a history of secret and forgotten corners of the Whoniverse. The first woman Doctors, the first black Doctor, animations, audios, stage plays and fan films.

The Fall of Atlantis – Page 198

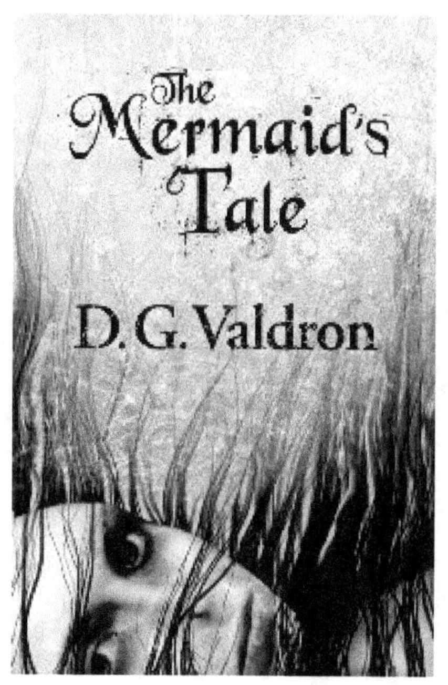

A Dark Fantasy of Murder and Redemption

There's a City where all the races come together uneasily, descending into civil war. There's a Mermaid, murdered cruelly her people distraught and crying out for justice. There's an Orc, her mission: Solve the murder, before it all comes crashing down. And something else... the world's first serial killer.

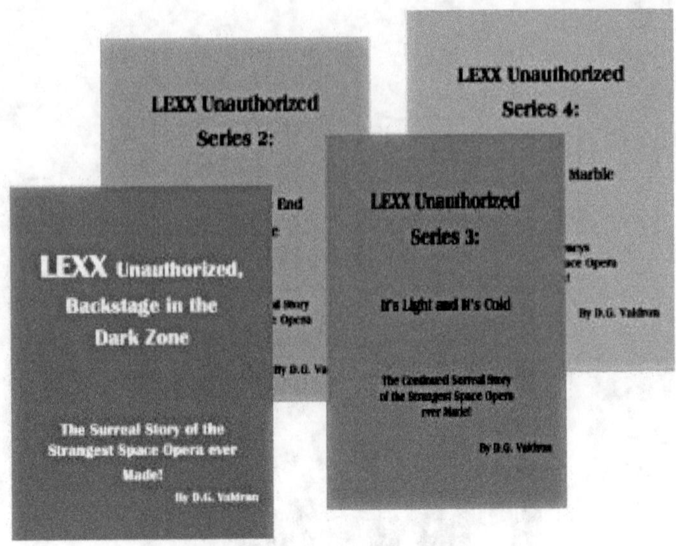

LEXX UNAUTHORIZED

LEXX Unauthorized about the making of a show about a giant space bug that blows up planets, the cowardly security guard who is its captain, and the undead assassin, runaway love slave, and robot head who form its crew.

Originally billed as 'Star Trek's Evil Twin,' the cultiest of cult sci fi, LEXX's forte was black humor, startling visuals, big ideas, and a sensibility that had more to do with surrealists like Jodorowsky or Bunuel than mainstream science fiction. And, as unconventional as it was onscreen, the story of how it came to be is even more bizarre.

STARLOST UNAUTHORIZED

And the Quest for Canadian Identity

The series that was Harlan Ellison's nemesis. The most controversial series in the history of sci fi television. This exhaustively researched book, based on interviews with some of the stars and writers, brings a fresh new interpretation of of the Starlost, and a re-evaluation of the series and its themes in the context of the 1970s crisis of Canadian nationalism.

The Fall of Atlantis – Page 201

TWILIGHT OF ECHELON

Published by

AT BAY PRESS

Based on the work of famed artist Robert Pasternak the book features paintings from Pasternak's Echelon series, accompanied by stories written independently by D.G. Valdron, Lovern Kindzierski, Alex Passey and Blaise Moritz.

The Fall of Atlantis – Page 202

www.ingramcontent.com/pod-product-compliance
Lightning Source LLC
Chambersburg PA
CBHW060447310726
48977CB00001B/354